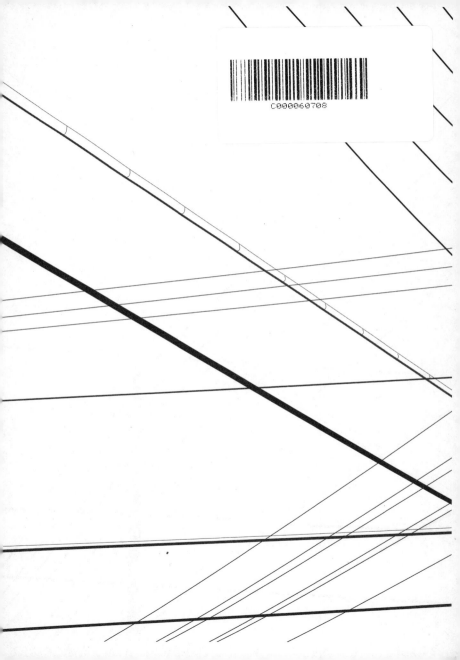

BOBBY NAYYAR was born in Handsworth, Birmingham in 1979. In 2006, he was published in the anthology *Mango Shake* (Tindal Street Press) as well as in journals such as *Wasafiri* and *Aesthetica*. He's been based in London since 2005, first in north London, now east. In October 2009 he founded Glasshouse Books. *West of No East* is his debut novel.

WEST OF NO EAST
While researching a photoessay on the first decade of the 21st century, Tarsem discovers a photograph of Rubina, a former university friend now working as a campaigner. Unable to comfort his wife who has just recovered from her second miscarriage, and cope with the spectre of restructure and redundancy at his office, he contacts her. In reconnecting he faces the prejudices of his youth. Tarsem is Sikh, Rubina is Muslim. And the last ten years have seen them follow opposing paths shaded by events beyond their control. Encouraged by her, Tarsem travels to India with his parents unaware of the impact it will have on all their lives.

WEST OF NO EAST

BOBBY NAYYAR

GLASSHOUSE
B O O K S

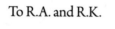
To R.A. and R.K.

KATRINA

We remember the pictures.

An obese black woman stands at the side of a concrete bridge pouring water into a styrofoam tray. She is wearing a white sleeveless T-shirt and maroon jogging bottoms soaked to the knee, her hair in a pony tail. Beside her a scrawny black and grey dog sits resigned and mute, a blue leash tying him to the white railing that runs alongside the edge of the bridge. Below them the dark water of the river is stippled with rain. A dead body dressed in a white plastic raincoat floats face down a few feet from them. In the instant the obese woman is forever engaged with the water pouring into the tray, while the world looks on in horror at what passes below.

Reid called my name. I turned in my seat and saw him standing in the doorway of his office. I don't know how long he had been watching me.

'What are you working on?' he asked, his arms folded.

'"The First Decade" piece,' I answered looking back at my computer screen. I opened some of the images I had collated over the last few weeks. He furrowed his brow, his face knotting, the onset of grey in his sideburns. He wasn't interested.

'Haven't you got more pressing things to do?'

I did. I lowered my head and blinked in acceptance. There were a number of gaps I had to fill, stock images to find, nothing that would press upon the fabric of the reader's consciousness like the images of Hurricane

Katrina, the 7/7 bombings or the fall of the World Trade Centre. I made an apologetic shrug and closed the photographs.

A pair of auditors, identically dressed in grey flannel suits, approached. Reid retreated into his office before they passed. It wasn't a good sign. They had been with us for over a week, occupying the boardroom, arriving before nine and leaving after eight each day, the blandness of their expressions betraying nothing of what was happening or what was to come.

I stood up to stretch my back, glancing round to see who was left in the office. Most of the people over thirty were still there, a cloud of uncertainty absorbing us all. It was hard to tell how much work was actually being done. I hope you never experience this for yourself, but most of office life is spent posturing. I was no different, yet finally I had a task that actually meant something to me, a photoessay that would carry my name. I looked to Reid's office, he was on a call, he said a few words into his mouthpiece then got up and closed his door. Left unwatched, I reopened the images for my essay.

Laid out on a computer screen the first decade of the twenty-first century didn't look so good. It was all too easy to find images of destruction and devastation, be it natural or manufactured.

'Find something fluffy,' I remember Johanna, the fashion editor, saying in a review meeting. 'We've had enough bombs to last a lifetime. Throw some bunnies in there.'

People laughed. Someone mentioned Lady Gaga in her meat dress, another asked for some Michael Jackson pics. Half the room ended up talking about *The X-Factor*. It was early November, a girl band had just been voted off. No one could remember their names.

I made eye contact with James, the arts editor.

'What about Obama's inauguration,' he asked, feeling my frustration that no one was taking my project seriously.

'You could do a split screen with Obama then and Obama after the mid-terms,' Johanna added.

People weren't sure if they were supposed to giggle or look concerned. Fenton, the editor-in-chief, flicked his wrist. The conversation moved on to another article. It was my second review meeting, the first time I had an article to bring to the table. I caught a sneer from Reid as I walked back to my desk. We were production editorial, we weren't editors, let alone creatives. He made a blithe comment to put me in my place, which I accepted with a thin smile, better to let him have it than throw more work at me. I was happy. I was somewhere he had never been.

But now I was in it. The last ten years were unwritten, there were no books to consult, no TV programmes to watch, my searches dotted along the decade. I focussed on the rise of extremism, I moved from dusty roads in Iraq and Afghanistan to the heartlands of England. One particular image caught my eye.

It was a Saturday in Birmingham, August 2009, the city centre caught in the middle of protests and counter-protests. On the one side young and middle-aged white male faces, jeering, arms aloft, some holding placards that say 'NO 2 ISLAM', others a banner: 'KEEP BRITAIN SAFE!'. Some of the faces convey a jocularity, others a passionate anger. It's hard to tell how many of them are there, and where they hope to go.

In between there is a small group of Asian youths. I couldn't place them in between the different crowds, I struggle to piece the images into one coherent jigsaw. I imagine they are at a distance, hooded and smiling, ready to recoil if things turn violent. Behind them pedestrians stand back and watch.

On the other side, a line of policemen barricade the anti-racism protesters. Some are white, some are Asian. I wonder why they are the ones being held back. Grouped together the photographs begin to lose their objectivity, my feelings start to sink in. It is then that I saw her. Near the front of the anti-racism protesters, a beautiful Asian face framed by a light blue, silk hajib, her hand stretching out in defiance. I zoomed in and cropped the image. It had been a decade but I was certain that it was her. Rubina, the first woman I ever loved.

As the years begin to pass with an alarming ease, it becomes harder to judge which memories you will hold on to. The events of your life changing like the seasons, like falling snow to drops of rain pattering against a window, which is too far to see. I don't know why, but when I tried to think of Rubina, the first memory that came to mind was our matriculation day photograph, way back in 1997.

Like a job interview, or office politicking, the paths of each student could be plotted from how they dressed to this most formal of events. The bell curve ran from the public school students whose dress, haircuts and posture put them in another decade, if not another century, to the rebel mathmo who pulled the finger at the wide-angle lens. I was somewhere in the middle in my Burton suit and blue gown, the upper working class-ness of it all confirmed by an undone top button, tie barely applying any pressure around my neck.

Rubina was one of the last people to arrive. She walked nervously onto the scene, the apology on her lips betrayed by the buoyancy in her eyes. Stood before one hundred people on a multi-tiered platform, seventy of them men, many of them pimpled and virginal, she was Venus to a wide range of Fools, her shoulder-length black hair in thick curls, olive skin and mahogany eyes, a white summer dress cut above the knee, tempered only by the dowdiness of her gown.

We were arranged alphabetically by surname, she was meant to be somewhere in the middle, while I was on the far right, closer to the ground. I watched as she walked up the rickety metal stairs and caught her eye as she passed. There was a pause, a registration, enough time for me to feel my cheeks flush red and for her to look demurely at her feet. We were both eighteen, Asian and away from home for the first time – cliched as it is, I made more of a connection in that split second than I had all week. I looked ahead, deep into the lens as it absorbed the world around me.

Anita wasn't at home. She had been back at work for less than a week. I expect she was trying her best to avoid the sympathy of her colleagues by overloading herself with work. I couldn't help but feel that she was avoiding me too. My role was simply to stay out of it. To support. To hold. To comfort and let the moments when her resolve weakened pass without comment. I had learned enough the first time around.

I took off my coat and shoes and lay down on the sofa. My eyes were stinging, I placed my index finger and thumb against my closed eyelids to feel the warmth of my skin, and my blood beneath. In the depth of that dark grey heat I once again pictured Rubina on that day on the cusp of autumn.

The regret of failed transgressions become more acute in married life. It isn't even a question of time, like something you grow out of, rather it's something you carry with you like a small stone in your shoe. I haven't really had that many, but in the past few months I had thought about a few of them quite deeply, but never about Rubina. I felt a sinking feeling in my stomach, got up and went to the spare room. We kept our unopened items in there, most of it my stuff. Anita gave up nagging me about it six months after we moved in, the stack of boxes having gained totem-like status.

I picked up the first box and tore away the sticky tape. It contained old copies of the magazine. When I started the job I assiduously kept hold of two copies, one to look at and one to store away. Now I didn't bother. The next box had my old photographs, many of them in the original envelopes from the photo developers, even old rolls of film in plastic cases. Most of them were from my childhood, only a few were from university. I remembered that I had gone through most of my photographs and letters and separated them into the things I would carry into my new life, and the ones I would leave at my parents' home. It was sad really, I didn't want to explain my past to Anita, and neither did she. I expected that the matriculation photograph was somewhere in a wardrobe back home.

I opened the third box feeling a nostalgic second wind. Upon sight of the white, clothbound hardback books I felt a rush of blood to my cheeks. They were my idea. I was determined not to have a typical Indian wedding with days upon days of camera footage cheesily edited together. Instead I convinced Anita, her parents and mine to let me use a photographer who often worked for the magazine. He'd document the wedding and put together a book we could give as gifts. On balance it turned out to be more expensive, and even though the photographs captured the wedding with a poetic grace and timeless realism, they missed the heart of the event, the heaving mass of people dancing, the furtive glances, the matchmaking and empty bottles of whisky.

I turned the pages not quite believing I was looking at myself only eighteen months ago. Anita looked beautiful, her dark brown hair tied up, immaculate makeup, her luminous almond brown eyes with flecks of green that reflected the gold spirals of her necklace. The photograph of us both seated in her parents' living room, surrounded by wailing relatives, as we were five minutes from making the ceremonial exit, became noted by my parents – in particular my mother – for one thing: Anita never shed a tear. The photographs missed her movements as she hugged her siblings, aunts and friends, tears only clinging to her cheek to test her foundation. She was dry, the soft steel of her resolve caught in every exposure.

Justine Evrard. They called her Joan of Arc. French, obviously, tall but not gangly, slim and well proportioned, she had the air of an athlete: perfect poise and balance as she sashayed around the office with just enough menace in her clear blue eyes. Always dressed in impeccable tailored suits, polished shoes and a silk scarf, Evrard's one concession to disorder was her untied shoulder length brown hair, which she toyed with when men made mistaken attempts to flirt with her. Everyone below a certain pay grade feared her, as she only ever came to the magazine when there were cuts to be made.

I felt her latest arrival deep in the pit of my stomach, like nausea on an empty stomach, nothing quite there to heave. Reid had been paying extra attention to me, maybe I was paranoid but in meetings I noticed him taking notes each time I spoke. It came as no surprise when I received a memo informing me that I was to have a meeting with Evrard and him at the end of the week. There was a hush over the office that day like someone had died. The ones who received memos trying their best to conceal it, the fear and disappointment clear in their faces.

I hadn't told anyone, not even Anita. Things were fragile enough between us, as we tried to return to some sort of routine where we essentially spent time together doing domestic chores, occasionally sharing a bottle of wine over dinner, talking about work but not really saying anything meaningful. I turned up for work on time and stared at the screen, replied to emails and made my necessary phone calls, letting everything else fall by the wayside.

I continued to hold on to my photoessay about the last ten years, steadfast in my belief to include part of December 2010 I missed the magazine's print deadline, much to Reid's disapproval. Feeling magnanimous Fenton sent me a kind email saying that we could run the piece on the website. I had a feeling he never planned to include it in the magazine anyway. It's one of the funny things I fear you'll discover about being put in your place: more often than not it's actually your own self-perceptions that end up failing you. I could have finished the piece countless times but I just couldn't do it.

I logged on to several photo libraries. I had to find an image for a comment piece on the Remembrance services. The commentator was as right-wing as the magazine got, when my first round of images of servicemen stood by the Cenotaph were sent back with the words 'find something edgier' I knew what he was aiming at. My gaze moved to west London and young, darkly clothed Asian men holding black flags. At their feet lay a large poppy engulfed in flames, slogans bearing the words EMPIRE and HELL. The narrowness of the picture made it hard to tell how many were really there, at least eight or nine, the point made, the damage done. What comes afterwards is a matter of personal choice. I could have sent more photos of servicemen, but resigned as I felt that day, I sent a couple of pics of these young men and their anger. I had ten minutes to go until my meeting.

—

'Please take a seat,' Evrard said.

Reid was sitting beside her. He uncrossed his arms and poured me a glass of water. We were in the boardroom, a rectangular room with large windows that looked out towards the South Bank, the sun having set leaving us beneath the glare of the ceiling lights. The room had been cleared of its regular tables, all that was left was Evrard's desk in the centre of the room, both of them sat behind it. I tried to quell the sensation in my stomach and took my seat on the other side, resolute to sit straight and hold firm.

'Now Tarsem you may be aware that we have been reviewing each and every one our processes in response to the financial downturn,' Evrard began. 'The year to date figures for the magazine are not good, and as we continue to invest in our digital output we unfortunately have to make efficiencies elsewhere.'

She paused. I leaned back.

'What does this mean for me?' I managed to say.

Reid opened his mouth to speak. Evrard cut in.

'Christopher, along with the other department heads, has been analysing the workflow of his team. Based upon his assessment I have identified where we could make time efficiencies.'

Evrard's delivery was flawless, just enough emotion without any trace of judgement in her voice. I made eye contact with her, the stillness of her deep blue eyes felt comforting.

'In your role Tarsem, we have identified that you are working at less than full capacity. I would like to propose that from next week onwards we trial a four-day working week.'

'What? You think I'm not busy enough to work five days a week?' I looked at Reid. 'Where did you get that from?'

Evrard looked at him. It was almost as if she had lost a bet.

'Tarsem, this is a good assessment of your work in the face of having to make some difficult decisions,' Reid said. He didn't have the same polish as Evrard. 'But it has been noted that over the last few months you've been wanting to expand your position and grow. In any other circumstance this would be welcomed, but now in this particular climate we simply cannot accommodate it.'

'What expansion?' I said, more out of the expectation that I would answer back than anything else. I knew what he was going to refer to. The least I wanted out of him was to say it.

He sipped some water. 'Like for example, the decade review piece that you still haven't finished.'

'But you agreed to give me that task.'

'And I expected it to be completed weeks ago.'

'Unfortunately, the bottom line is that we must make this change now or face even tougher decisions down the line,' Evrard said, the pitch of her voice rising ever so slightly.

I looked behind her to the framed prints of magazine covers from our heyday, every smiling face and beautiful figure bringing the promise of happiness, a window to a glorious past.

'What if I want to stay working a five-day week?'

'Then we would have to begin a consultation process to identify which possible role or roles you could perform to justify the extra day. During the process you would still be expected to work the four-day week.'

I slouched. The blood had drained from my cheeks leaving me feeling cold and depleted. Evrard tried to smile, careful not to make it seem like she was happy.

'As I said this is a temporary measure that will be reviewed on three-monthly basis. We're all having to make adjustments through this difficult period.'

We were told constantly that we were all in this together, but I had never felt so alone.

'When does this come into effect?' I asked, breaking eye contact.

Evrard leaned forward, I caught the scent of her perfume, it reminded me of lavender and jasmine.

'From today.'

After eighteen months of marriage it amazed me that Anita would still get dressed in the bathroom, or occasionally in our bedroom, always careful to keep her back turned towards me. It was late morning, a triangular opening where the drawn curtains met, which projected a sad grey light on the opposing wall. It was cold. It had been cold for a few days, the cloudiness of the sky and the swirling biting winds indicative of a coming snow, which of course no one would truly be prepared for. I lay in bed, duvet pulled up to my chin, inching across to the middle of the bed to take advantage of Anita's vacant space. She left a different kind of warmth, soft and fragrant with the creams she applied before going to sleep, cocoa butter and aloe. It was a reassuring warmth that reminded me that as distant as we often were, we were never completely alone.

Anita came into the room, a large towel wrapped around her, her long black hair dripping wet, a smaller towel in her hands. She looked at me before sitting at the edge of the bed to dry her hair.

'Aren't you getting up?' she asked.

I stretched my arms out and yawned. 'Too cold.'

'I put the heating on. Come on get ready. I'll make breakfast then we can go shopping.'

'I can't.'

She stopped rubbing her hair, turned and looked at me.

'I've got to go to Hornchurch. Mum's not well.' I lied. 'I'll clean up before I go. Sorry.'

'Are you going to stay the night?'

'No. You know what she gets like. I just need to go, have a cup of tea, do a couple of things around the house and then she'll be happy, and I can come back.'

I saw the colour of Anita's face change, darken as her reserves swelled, she was too tired to fight, she dismissed everything I had said with the rising and lowering of her eyebrows, a sigh escaping to the ether. The next few moments passed in silence. I don't know what spurred her, but Anita decided to dress in the room. Damp hair around her shoulders, she glanced over her shoulder to see if I was watching, a mischievous look in her eyes.

There had been times like this before, months ago, when things had been better. Games we'd play to break the monotony. Anita wasn't afraid of sex or her body. She was beautiful, soft light skin that gave the appearance of a woman in her early twenties, five foot three or four, she took good care of herself, secretly hoping I would too without much coercion. It wasn't modesty that kept her naked body away from me, it was a belief that there was an order to maintain, that the law of diminishing returns applied as easily to people as it did to things.

She loosened the large towel revealing her delicate shoulder blades and the curve of her spine, the contours of her body extending to her hips. She hadn't exercised for a few weeks, conscious of any accumulation, she put on her underwear with the towel still wrapped around her waist, glancing at me once again, her left breast exposed. This would normally be the point where I would concede, agree to whatever was planned, we'd hold each other silently for a few minutes, our bodies perfectly aligned, breathing each other's air, our heartbeats slowing to meet each other. Sometimes we would take our time, stopping to talk, to understand each other, other times it would be quick and heated like a summer storm, something distinctively dark at its root.

On that day I did nothing. I lay back and watched. Confused, Anita hastened, putting on the rest of her clothes without looking back. Fully dressed, she stood at the foot of the bed, her luminous brown eyes moist with the dew of tears.

'I haven't been well,' I said to break the silence. Again another lie that wasn't so far from the truth.

'Maybe it's a good thing that you're going to see your mother,' she said, a hint of derision in her voice. She didn't want to argue. She touched my foot through the duvet then left the room.

I took the train to Hornchurch. I didn't want to drive. I just wanted to drift and watch the blur of suburban houses and leadening sky. I still hadn't told Anita that I was working a four-day week. It had been a fortnight since it happened. The first Friday I woke as normal, dressed and had breakfast, leaving at my usual time. I treated it like a day off, strolled around the National Gallery, ate in the corner of a Chinese restaurant not far from Leicester Square and then watched film. I was home later than usual, telling Anita that I had an urgent assignment that had to be done, the lie compounding. I counted the cost of that day – it was far too expensive, much more than I would spend normally.

The second Friday was far more parsimonious. The realisation hit that my monthly salary would be a few hundred pounds lighter, and that there was little I could do to hide it from Anita once our direct debits went out at the end of the month. I got up as usual, left the house before her and walked to the DLR station. The slow chug of the train gave me time to think. The lie would be up before Christmas. Anita would comb through our expenses and make cuts, our marriage would suffer another setback.

I got off at Bank and walked among the suited. Everyone rushing to be somewhere, sparking along the spokes of the City. Sad as it was, I would have given anything to be with them. There is something to be said of the media life, the parties and the gloss, the rise in your friends' eyebrows when you mention whichever celebrity was in the office. At the end of it all, the print rubs off and all you really need is enough money to make it through the month, save just enough to give you enough hope that your life is worth more than just the sum of its parts. Deep in this funk, I sat in a greasy cafe drinking cheap coffee, rehearsing what I would say to my wife.

Mother was making tea when I arrived, the kitchen infused with the scent of cardamom and cloves. She was wearing an old yellow salwar kameez and a cream cardigan, her feet exposed in flimsy plastic sandals. She wasn't surprised to see me.

'I thought you would come today,' she said hugging me. 'Do you want some tea, there's enough for two.'

I took off my coat and shoes and sat in the living room. There's something you should know about me – I am an only child. Over the years the story as to why have varied, the best I have is that my birth created a complication that meant that mother couldn't have any more children. I was the only only Asian child in my junior school and all the way up to university. I sought for brothers and sisters in friends, but it never quite worked out, people found me too detached. Whenever they came to my home, they added vain and conceited to the list. The living room alone had five framed photographs of me, charting my progress from toddler to graduate. I sat and stared at my former selves. Mother brought the tea and sat beside me.

'Where's dad?'

'He's working. Anita?'

'Shopping.'

She told me off for not helping my wife, then placed her hand on mine, a thin smile on her face. We sat in silence drinking the tea. I fidgeted and muttered to myself. There was something I had wanted to tell her for weeks.

'What's the matter beta?' she said, sitting away from me so she could see my face clearly.

'It's Anita. She had another miscarriage.'

'Again? When.'

'A couple of months ago.'

'Why didn't you tell me.'

Truth was Anita didn't want her to know. The first time it happened, my mother and mother-in-law stayed at the flat to look after her. I knew it was a bad idea but went along with it, as I needed all the help I could get. Anita was unconsolable. There was a coldness in her eyes when I spoke to her. We had only been married for six months, we knew each other well enough to have a baby but not enough to lose one. I was too awkward around her, I hid my grief. When mother found out that her peer was staying at the flat, she demanded to come too. I let it happen, more for my benefit than Anita's. I needed the comfort of her arms.

But on the third day the comfort and consolation broke down. The two mothers fought. What started as idle talk, old wives' tales and astrology as to why this had happened soon turned to the matter that had rankled both sets of parents since we met: Anita and I were from different castes. We were both Sikh, but she was a Jat, while I was a Chamaar, an Untouchable. Both mothers claimed that the other had said our difference in caste was the reason why Anita miscarried. I had preferred the hocus pocus explanations. I believed my mother, while Anita believed hers. An old wound reopened, which in some strange way distracted us enough to help the new wound heal. The weeks became months, we got help, our parents made a cursory reconciliation. Now we were back. I could see the consternation in my mother's face.

'This marriage,' she started before getting up to leave the room.

'"This marriage" what?'

Some words don't need to be said. I leaned back and stared at myself as a baby, round, fat cheeks, knitted jumper and nappies, crawling on the lino, transfixed by the camera lens, the high pitched sound as the flash warmed up and covered me in a bright light forever reflected in the corner of my deep brown eyes.

The first time I spoke to Rubina was at a formal hall put on to welcome the new students. We were told that formal hall was a special three-course dinner held a few times a week. We would have to wear our gowns and be on our best behaviour as the Master of the college would be attending. I followed a group of freshers from my halls of residence, waited with them while they bought bottles of wine. In those days I didn't drink alcohol. It was a resolve that dissolved within a few weeks, as I found that there were enough things about me that made me socially awkward, sobriety didn't have to be one of them.

The Great Hall was magnificent – a high vaulted ceiling, a raised section at the end of the room where the Fellows would eat carefully watched by a painting of the College's founder, Henry VIII. The students would sit at one of the four rows of wooden tables, the wood-panelled walls adorned with paintings of the former Masters. The magnificence of the room was somewhat unsettled by the presence of the uniformed serving staff, women dressed in black and white pinafores, men in white shirts and navy blue blazers. It gave the appearance of a life still rooted in feudalism, with the students soon to form their cliques along the fault lines that divide this country.

I saw Rubina as I entered the room. She was standing by the wall on the the left side of the room. I shuffled and squeezed my way ahead of the others so I could take the seat directly opposite to her. She made eye contact, flashed the briefest of smiles, which masked a sigh of relief. A pair of mathematicians had taken the seats to her left and right. They were working like a tag team, boasting about the wine they had bought and threatening to penny her wine glass throughout the dinner. She outstretched her arm.

Now there are many things that I should apologise for – most will come with time – but this is one of my deepest regrets. I took Rubina's hand with the emotion of a man falling in love, the softness of her skin, her warmth mingling with my own. I felt the heat rising against my skin, a lightness in my stomach.

'Hi, I'm Rubina,' she said revealing a perfect set of white teeth.

I felt my heart sink. I couldn't control it. I knew at that instant that she was a Muslim. In the rank of my prejudices, it would have been better if she were a Buddhist, a black woman, a born again Christian with platinum blonde hair and crystal blue eyes. I remembered the apocryphal stories of relatives who had partnered with Muslims, their subsequent disownment, rumours of their new names, never to be seen again. Rubina caught the edge of my disappointment.

'Most people call me Ruby,' she added, withdrawing her hand.

'I'm Tarsem. Some people call me Tarzan on account of my sterling physique.'

'Really?'

'Really. This isn't the most flattering of gowns.'

We sat down, the mathmos poured their wine while the staff served the first course. Rubina told me she was reading Social and Political Sciences. She was originally from Birmingham, the youngest of three. Both of her brothers worked in the family business: a cash and carry supermarket in

Balsall Heath. From an early age she was determined to go to university. Her parents were supportive. The only stipulation they made was that she was to go to Birmingham University if she didn't get into Cambridge or Oxford.

'And what's your story?' she asked while taking a sip of wine. She noticed that I was only drinking water but made no comment.

'Well, I guess my parents are a lot like yours. They wanted me to stay in London but I persuaded them that we all have to make sacrifices in the pursuit of a better education,' I said as one of the serving staff placed the main course of pheasant, roast potatoes, carrots and peas in front of me. Rubina stifled a laugh.

'So what are you: medicine, economics or law?'

'Don't be so cliched.'

'What then?'

'History of Art.'

'History of Art! How'd you swing that?'

'I've always been passionate about art and images, so I told my parents that I'd have the best chance of being successful if I followed my passions into academia, and then transferred those qualifications into a career.'

'Well, bravo for that. What did your siblings say?'

'I don't have any siblings.'

'Really?'

'Yes, really. Why does nobody ever believe me when I say that?'

'Sorry,' Rubina leaned a little closer towards me, which attracted the attention of one of the spurned mathmos. 'It's 'cos you don't seem like the only child type.'

The mathmo made his move and dropped a penny in Rubina's glass of red. It was the second time he had done it that evening. She flashed him a reproachful glance, which soon melted into a playful punch on the arm. I felt the first twinge of envy, the rush of blood to my cheeks confirming that even though my prejudices could cause my heart to sink, they couldn't stop it from resurfacing. Rubina held her glass aloft.

'To only children.'

She downed the glass in one painful movement, deposited the coin on the mathmo's plate, before falling back into her seat. She reached across and took my glass of water.

'I think this lady's had her fill.'

The night was clear over Great Court, a crescent moon and a dusting of stars across the sky. It was the perfect surroundings to be young, troubled and falling in love. Rubina managed to dispatch of the mathmos. They were insistent that we join them in the cramped College bar. Rubina refused, exclaiming that if she drank anymore she'd end up vomiting on one of them. They tipped their cap at me like I had played a shrewd hand by not drinking, quietly certain that it was another case of the coloured ones sticking together. I wasn't so sure. Rubina had already started tiptoeing her way on the cobbled paving. I received a shove in the back to point me in the right direction. I caught up with her.

'I probably shouldn't be saying this but I was wondering if you were going to come after me,' she said, linking her arm with mine to help her balance. 'You can walk me to my room. Sounds old fashioned doesn't it?'

'Nothing wrong with that. Where do you live?'

'Blue Boar. You?'

'Wolfson.'

We walked up some stairs and entered her block. She let go of my arm and fumbled for her keys.

'This is me,' she said, her back straightened, both of us made tense by our proximity. It was a crossroads moment. A step forward and my whole life would have been different. Rubina opened her door, I remained unmoved. We both understood each other with a smile. This time the door would close. The next time she would invite me in.

For the first few seconds I thought I was at home with Anita. The realisation sinking like a tablet in water as I glanced around the room I grew up in, half expectant of a call for me to hurry up and get dressed. Moving from child to man I remembered my first evening with Rubina. I rummaged in one of my cupboards, removing envelopes of photographs until I could pull out the long matriculation photograph. I opened the curtains, the condensation laden windows revealing a grey sky punctuated by green treetops. It didn't take me long to find Rubina's face amongst the crowd, her radiant smile and bright eyes bringing back memories of then contrasted with now. I remembered the image of her in the crowd of protesters: strong, defiant, the same brightness burning but also a maturity, perhaps augmented by the covering of her hair. It amazed me. People have been covering their hair for millennia, yet it still managed to inspire a sense of otherness and displacement inside me. Naive as it sounds, I wanted to get to the root of that thought and pull it out. Above all I knew I wanted to see Rubina again.

I dressed and went downstairs. Father was alone in the living room watching one of the Asian news channels. He sat transfixed as a report unfolded on a kidnap and extortion case in Ludhiana. The style of reporting wasn't so far from the tabloid news channels in the UK: light on content, heavy on repeating the same details with footage of the poor victim seemingly in a loop. I could only really understand the gist of what had happened, admittedly my Punjabi isn't that strong, something I have always regretted but never had the compulsion to fix. Instead I focussed on my father.

Father had been working for the Royal Mail since he was nineteen – well over thirty years. It was a concept seemingly lost in time, probably around the 80s, when the idea of a long and fulfilling pension seemed to fritter and fall into the sea. I don't know how he had lasted through the years of recession and reorganisation, where his job was only a statistic in some accountant's spreadsheet. I thought I could tell him about my work problems, but I knew deep down that he would be disappointed. No matter the mitigating circumstances, he would see my four-day week as a personal failure.

An advertisement break started. Father scratched his grey stubble and then looked at me. From the look in his eyes I understood that mother had told him about Anita's miscarriage.

'Why did you stay the night?' he asked, a hint of anger in his voice.

'I wasn't feeling well. I just wanted a night on my own. I know it sounds silly.'

'You should be with your wife.' He put a bit more stress on the final word. Ever since we got married father had used the word 'wife' instead of 'Anita'. It was like he didn't want to personalise it, it was just a term or a euphemism for something else.

'I guess mum told you.'

He blinked an answer and repeated that I should be with her. I don't think that either one of us wanted to discuss my marriage, so I decided to fall back by talking about work. Working at the magazine was one of the few things that father had supported me in.

'Well, to tell the truth, I've been having a hard time at work.'

'What happened?'

'They cut me down to a four-day week.'

'What?' he reached for the remote and turned the volume down. 'Did you do something?'

I rolled my eyes, 'I didn't do anything. The magazine's been going down the pan for years. The circulation keeps dropping, website figures go up, but advertising revenue goes down. First they squeezed us into a smaller office, now they're making cuts across the board.'

'Is that why you came here? Did you have a fight?'

'With Anita? No, not about this.' I paused, 'I haven't told her yet.'

He tutted and puffed out his cheeks. He was in relatively good shape, but in recent years the skin on his face had started to sag. For many years you believe that your father is invincible, but one day you realise that he is just a man, and another that he has grown old. He scratched his head.

'Don't tell your mother. She didn't want you to do that job in the first place. But you have to tell your wife.'

'I know. She isn't easy to talk to at the best of times. I've just been trying to pick the right moment. We've had enough bad news for one year.'

'Are you OK for money?'

I nodded feeling like I was a teenager again, forever asking for a bit more. 'I just need to find some freelance work or something to fill the gap. It's possible.'

'Well do it.'

I took that as encouragement and motioned to get up. Uncharacteristically, father held his hand out and stopped me.

'There's something else,' he said. He gritted his teeth, the pitch of his voice dropping like it had been pulled down by the gravity of the situation. 'Your mother and I will be going to India next year.'

'What for?'

'I've decided it's time to build the house.'

He should have called it The House. Father had talked about it since I was a child. He had a large plot of land in his village in the Punjab. I have vague memories of seeing it when I was thirteen, the only time I had been in India. His dream was simple: to build a house when it was time to retire and his children (sadly, child) had children of his own. Life hadn't gone to plan. I thought he would have waited a few more years.

'So are you going to retire?'

He nodded. 'Not yet of course. There's a lot of planning and legal things to do over there. Why don't you come with us?'

'To India? It's not exactly the best time. Anita wouldn't want to be cooped up.'

We both understood that the 'with mother' was implied. Father touched my hand in a rare gesture of tenderness.

'Why don't you just come? Your mother and I are going for a month. You could join us for a week, maybe two. We'll pick you up and drop you off in Amritsar. There's a lot of things I never got to show you last time. When was it?'

'1993 I think. What do you want to show me?'

'Lots of things. We could go to Shimila, Delhi, treat it like a real holiday.'

It was amazing. I had never seen him so animated. My father and I had never been that close. I think he always dreamed of having a big family, each child becoming something different, something special. Despite my academic endeavours, I didn't feel like I was the child/son he had wanted.

When I was at school, I found myself looking for father figures in my teachers. This felt like a rare opportunity to actually get to know him.

'When are you planning to go?'

'February.'

'When do you need an answer from me?'

'You've got until Christmas to decide.'

As a simple coda he turned up the volume of the TV. The news report still dwelling on the lurid details of the kidnapping in Ludhiana. I had a few weeks to decide. I felt another crossroads opening up before me.

After all corporate talks and culling, the office returned to some state of normalcy. There was a steady hum of keyboard tapping, the occasional muted ring of a telephone, a mixture of relief and denial that we were one or two restructures away from folding. I had adapted to my four-day week, the loss of eight hours injecting a sense of urgency into each day, which faded once the sun set around three thirty. The darkness outside compounded by the dimness of the energy efficient lightbulbs inside. We were in a state of collective depression, afraid to call its name. But as we crept closer to the end of a terrible year, there was at least some flickers of resistance in the world outside.

I had to find a good photograph of the protests that had taken place over the weekend. 'Protest' wasn't really a word that sat well in the English lexicon. I remembered the protests at Cambridge: five students standing outside a closed faculty building with a lank, makeshift banner, the feeling that in five or so years' time they would be working in an investment bank or a barrister's chambers. This was different. It was organised, it was national and it provoked a response.

Thirty young people sat on the pavement outside a department store, some of them holding small A4 banners about tax avoidance, a line of fluorescent-yellow-jacketed policemen behind and in front of them. It wasn't really clear if the police were there to protect the protesters or the store owned by the tax evader. There was a hint of resignation in the faces of the young men and women sat on cold concrete. And although the photograph lacked the narrative impact of the classic images of protest – Thich Quang Duc's burning body on a street in Vietnam, or the unknown student stood before a queue of tanks in Tiananmen Square – there was still a story told in their faces. The sense that they were inheriting a world they would not accept. A sense that change was always possible no matter how bleak things were.

I thought of Rubina stood in the crowd of protesters in Birmingham, her hand reaching out, her face as youthful as a decade ago. The main difference being the depth of her mahogany eyes, which concealed an anger mixed with sorrow. And then there was the hijab. The garment had pulled me in like a riptide. I hope you can forgive me of this but I never thought that Rubina would become a practising Muslim. She was so much of a free spirit at university, philosophically so, it wasn't just about drinking or smoking or going out with boys. In the one conversation we did have about religion – more than anything to confirm that I was a Sikh and she was a Muslim – she told me that her parents expected certain things, but wanted her to go beyond the ground they had treaded and create something new. In that we were no different.

Ten years ago I fixated on what she was, now I fixated on what she wore. The doubt beginning to creep in that I was no more enlightened than the thugs who threatened her on that day in Birmingham. I don't know if it was the compulsion to understand and counter my own prejudices, or the fact that the love and desire I felt for Rubina had never really gone away. Either way I felt an urgent need to see her, as if my understanding of myself and my future somehow depended on her. I looked over my shoulder to see if Reid was around. His door was closed.

It didn't take me long to find her: two words entered in a search engine, a trawl through a few webpages to find out where she worked, some tagged images of her at various functions, a little bit of cross referencing just to be sure. Rubina was working at a charity that specialised in race and equality. Her work profile listed a number of awards for various campaigns, as well as her email address. She had a sizeable footprint on the web, far eclipsing my own, a touch of web envy setting in. Dismissing this I started to compose an email to her, picking my words with care, feeling that each sentence would be assessed, pondered and judged. I mentioned that I had seen a photograph of her, threw in as casually as possible that I was married. The word inevitably bringing me to Anita, her doe eyes clearly aware of the chasm between us. In a different life it would have been something I mentioned to her, perhaps over dinner, just to make sure she was aware, not to make it seem like I was asking for her permission or anything. I still had to tell her about my work situation, the possibility of a trip to India, and now my attempts to get in touch with an old, female friend. The pieces of news stacking like planes in the air, circling, running on empty, but still not wanting to land.

It was the night after the violence. What started as a protest quickly becoming a riot from Westminster all along to Oxford Street. Students hurling bottles filled with paint, defacing monuments and tearing flags. Horses charging in, policemen with batons raised high, protesters pinned by incumbent knees. It didn't feel like England: such a chill in the air, electricity surging through the streets, sirens streaming westwards, an endless trail of blue light. The morning newspapers were dominated by a photograph of a royal couple trapped in their car, white paint across the bodywork, a look of horror and sheer panic on their faces, bulletproof glass and reinforced steel keeping the country an inch from revolution. If ever there was a night when we were 'all in this together' it was then.

I walked along the Strand, turned right by the Zimbabwean Embassy and headed along William IV street. I was going to meet Rubina for a drink. She had replied almost instantly to my email, exclaiming that it was so wonderful that I had got in touch, and that she had been thinking about contacting me for quite a while. I ignored that statement – considering that it had been ten years – and wrote back to her suggesting we meet. There was a pause at this point, both of us thinking what this meant, and what it could be, I had made it clear that I was married, living in Wapping, she didn't mention a boyfriend or husband, I didn't ask. She replied saying that she was going to the theatre on Friday and could meet me for a drink beforehand. Friday, my fake work day. She confirmed a time and place. I agreed.

Anita had tried to talk to me the night before. I had made dinner and washed up, no doubt feeling guilty for a range of things. We sat and watched coverage of the riots on the TV, the volume turned down low. She leaned across and put her head on my shoulder, I could smell the scent of her perfume and conditioner. I repositioned myself and stretched out my left arm to hold her. There was bound to be a conversation coming, we contented ourselves to remain silent for a few minutes.

'Do you think we need to go back to counselling?' she asked in a half whisper.

I bit my lip for a few seconds, 'I know we're not in the place we expected us to be, but that doesn't mean that we need someone to tell us something's wrong.'

'So you admit that something's wrong?'

'Well, there are things that could be better between us, that doesn't take much explaining.'

'I feel like you keep things from me.'

I blushed, repositioned, Anita sat up, her face a few inches from mine. We looked at each other eye to eye for the first time in weeks. I kissed her. An impulsive kiss, like an leap into the unknown.

'Why don't we go out?' I said, secretly pleased that she hadn't rejected my kiss.

'Out? Like on a date?'

'Yeah, why not. Dinner and a movie? We haven't done something like that in ages.'

'How about tomorrow?'

I dry swallowed and remembered my appointment with Rubina. It was stupid: the belief, however remote, that a quick drink with her would somehow develop into something longer, dinner, a change of venue, a nightcap. This is what it means to be a man. Unfortunately.

'Is Friday no good?'

I mumbled my way through an answer, explained that there was a work function and I had no idea of how long it would last. Anita pouted, then leaned against me, pleased at least that we were comfortable in each other's arms.

Now I was sat at a small table in the corner of a wine bar trying my best not to stare anxiously at the entrance. I had butterflies in my stomach, hadn't felt like that in years, the unease reminding me that I would have to make conversation, be amiable and mindful of my appearance. Rubina arrived fifteen minutes late. She approached, an apologetic wave of her hand, a broad and genuine smile. I stood, we passed an awkward moment of not knowing whether to kiss or shake hands, settled on a shoulder hug. She took off her gloves and coat to reveal a stunning office dress with matching trousers, no doubt inspired by the salwar kameez. Her hijab was jade-coloured with golden, embroidered flowers. We sat, she ordered sparkling water in contrast to my glass of red.

'So here we are,' Rubina said to break the silence. We had both taken a few seconds to contemplate each other's faces, to see what the last ten years had done to us. She was as beautiful as I remembered, a few extra lines defining her cheeks, skin a little darker perhaps, the covering of her hair accentuating her deep, mahogany eyes. 'Please show me the photograph.'

'Oh yes,' I said reaching into my backpack. I had printed the photo of her at the protest in Birmingham. I placed it on the table, she snatched it, laughed, and covered her mouth with her right hand.

'I look like a revolutionary thug,' she said blushing.

'Looks like you were holding your own.'

'I had to. It really was a grim day,' her eyes danced towards mine. 'Can I keep it? I'll show my mum next time I'm in Brum.'

'Sure. How is your family?'

Her eyes lowered, 'My mum's fine. My father passed away nearly four years ago now.'

'I'm sorry.'

Rubina's right hand was resting on the table. I thought about touching it. I couldn't trace the root of the feeling, whether it was sympathy or merely compulsion. The moment passed.

'Cancer. The most devastating thing. I quit my job and went back to Birmingham. Dad tried his best all the way. It changed all of our lives, mine, mum's, Mo and Kam's. After, I went with mum to Pakistan to grieve. We spent three months there, a lot of time with his relatives. They wanted to show me the places he never could, where he was born, where he grew up. It's when I started wearing this.' She touched her head, her right hand moving away from me. 'I noticed you staring at it. I get that a lot with old uni friends. Like I've descended from another planet.'

'I didn't mean to stare,' I said, my voice shrinking. 'It's just that … It's just, well, I don't know how to put it.'

'Let me help: you never thought that Rubina Khan would wear the hijab – the most oppressive garment on the planet.' Her sarcasm was softened by the warmth of her mahogany eyes.

'No,' I defended, 'OK maybe a little. I mean it did come as a surprise when I saw you in the photo.'

'I made a change. The way this country has turned in the last ten years facilitated it, in a strange roundabout way. We've been raised to be open, to adapt, but ultimately to conform and accept the world as seen through print and television. But it isn't like that. When I went to Pakistan, I saw a different world. A world that wasn't riddled with radicalism, some fucked up things for sure, but no different to anywhere else. I saw people. And I began to understand that – for want of a better word – the 'West's' representation of the 'East' was chimeric, so much so that it didn't exist, like a child covering his eyes, believing the world only exists when he sees it.' She laughed. 'Jeez. I'm starting to sound like I'm back at Cambridge. I mean you must have felt it yourself, the feeling that the East is being compressed, reduced year by year.'

'I'm not really sure. I do believe that ever since 9/11 opinions have become more and more polarised, perhaps even to the extent that we can look at 9/11 as a pivot, one world pre-9/11 and another one afterwards.'

'Yes, but that's a very western point of view. Travel and time off has given me the opportunity to actually listen to people, and get different perspectives. When was the last time you were in India?'

'Nearly twenty years ago, when I was at school.'

'You should go again. Cliched as it sounds, you do have roots there. When I came back from Pakistan I realised that I felt much more comfortable like this than I had ever done.'

'My parents are going in February next year. They asked me if I want to go.'

'You must. It's one of the things I regret. I never got the opportunity to spend proper time with my dad in Pakistan. That kind of time is more precious than anything, believe me.' She took a sip of water, I drank some wine. 'I've been rabbiting on, what about you?' Rubina reached across and touched my ring finger, 'So you're married to—'

'Anita.'

'Tell me about her. Was it an arranged or a "love" marriage?'

I looked at the dark surface of my wine, the reflection shifting and unbalanced. It was probably the last thing I wanted to discuss with Rubina, but I looked up and saw an eagerness in her eyes. And, in some perverse way, I knew that whatever I'd say would define the next steps of our relationship.

Every marriage has a story, even ours. A couple of years ago I was living in Stepney. Things were going well for me at the magazine, even though it was self-evident that we were in terminal decline. Even so I had been given a small promotion, taking on more responsibility for the print edition, having worked solely on the website. Reid rewarded me with his invitation to a journalism awards ceremony at the O2. It was a black tie affair, open bar, I'd be sitting with a few of the directors, as well as Fenton, who was unlikely to turn up unless he knew he was going to win something. At that time it felt like confirmation that I was on the up.

Anita was working as a publicist then. She had been invited by one of her authors, a well known critic – chronic letch – who had taken the plunge and written his sob story memoir, lauded by his mates but launched into obscurity with sales of a few hundred copies. Anita went because he was a valuable asset to the company, often reviewing their books with choice quotes that looked good on front covers. I first saw her waiting at the bar during an intermission. It was the beginning of summer, a general sense of relief in the air. Anita was wearing a vintage sleeveless, red, belted dress. She called it her torch song. It wasn't hard for her to stand out among the usual slinky black dresses. Her hair was short then, almost like a boy's, exposing a slender neck, the shape of her body a near perfect hour glass. It was clear that she had a few admirers, a couple of older, white men who would have known better if they weren't already bladdered.

From the silence and blank stares of the directors, I quickly realised why Reid had given me his seat: it was just another opportunity to put me in my place. And rather than play the yessum, who would speak only when spoken to and be happy just to be there, I decided to spend as much time possible away from the table. I stood back and watched Anita for a few moments, waiting for a space to open up beside her. We were the only two Asians at the bar. I was wearing a black tuxedo rented from Moss Bros with a rather sad looking clip on bow tie.

Anita looked at me and smiled when I stood beside her. I ordered a dry martini, not being sure what that meant but thinking that it might impress her. I fiddled with my tie while I waited, trying to think of something to say to strike up a conversation with her.

'Is that the kind that spins round and round?' she said, an edgy grin on her face.

'Depends on how much I've had to drink.'

We exchanged first names and where we worked, both of us impressed with the headway we were making in our publishing houses. There was a few seconds of registration, as we both realised that we were Punjabis, no rings on our fingers and a world of drinks in front of us. Anita had large catlike eyes that were a tender brown. She was attractive but not at first beautiful.

'So why are you hiding out here?' I asked, sipping cautiously at my martini.

'I'm supposed to be babysitting one of my authors.' She leaned in closer thinking that people might overhear. I could smell the alcohol on her breath, 'I hate him. He's started patting me on the bottom. Whenever he does it, I leave him alone so he knows he's on the naughty step. I so hope he doesn't win tonight.'

I told her about the cold shoulder from the directors. She sighed for both of us and said that it was the same everywhere, that every black and Asian person that had gone before her had said that you have to work twice as hard to be recognised as half as good. A call sounded for the final session of the awards.

'Where are you sitting?' Anita asked, touching my lapel. I pointed my table out. 'I'm over there. Look out for me,' she said walking away, glancing back over her left shoulder, the same look I grew accustomed to when we married.

As the evening progressed, we spent more and more time exchanging glances. Under the soft lights and shade the images we saw of each other were made complete by our expectations of how the night could end, alcohol, and the various schemes and plots our parents had been putting us through. I was thirty, Anita was twenty seven, both of us under increasing pressure to meet with prospective partners and go down the arranged marriage route. It was nothing new but it lacked the element of fate, which was something we had been craving for.

Anita's lecherous author won his award, she shot me a despairing glance and lowered her hand, her fingers beckoning me over. She told me afterwards that the author was angling for a threesome with her and his longterm partner, clearly he felt deserving after winning another pat on the back from his peers. The final award was given, the lights began to brighten, I took it as my cue to say goodnight to the people who had ignored me all evening and head over towards her.

The man – late forties, sandy blonde flop of hair, red-rimmed eyes with a veinous bulb of a nose – saw my approach. He responded by puffing out his chest, his head rocking like a stag about to charge. He was trying to get Anita to leave with him. She wasn't having any of it.

'Richard, let me introduce you to my dear friend—'

'Tarsem,' I interjected. 'Pleased to meet you.'

I offered my hand knowing he wouldn't take it. He actually was contemplating hitting me, his fingers forming into a fist. He muttered that they should be getting on.

Anita feigned contriteness, 'I'm so sorry. I meant to say that Tarsem and I had made plans to catch up. We haven't seen each other for quite some time.'

I nodded and touched her arm, 'We should be going or we'll never get a taxi.'

The older man acquiesced with a shrug of his shoulders. He clasped Anita, kissing her on both cheeks twice, his fingers pressing down and feeling the edge of her buttocks. She grabbed a white cashmere cardigan. We started to walk, she took my arm like she had known me all her life, and then for some unknown reason we started to run. Past the staggering, middle-aged men and women, the pompous, prettified younger women who stared and shot daggers as we giggled our way past them. We weaved and dodged, made it to the taxi rank without stopping, unable to wheeze as we were too busy laughing.

Anita stood close to me, less than an inch between us. Her eyes soft and vulnerable as she looked up at me.

'What shall we do?'

It was past eleven, the sky still bright, a warm wind circling around us.

'I doubt there will be anywhere worth going to around here. We could get a taxi and head west.'

'Where do you live?'

'Stepney.'

'Oh,' she said, slightly disappointed. 'I live in Wapping. Why don't we catch a taxi there?'

I nodded, careful not to look too keen or make it seem like the night was a foregone conclusion. We waited in silence for a black taxi to come, the tension starting to creep in between us.

'I don't do one night stands,' Anita said, looking up at the crescent moon.

'Neither do I,' I replied, which was true, but probably for completely different reasons. A taxi came, feeling slightly more confident Anita said her address, we both sat back, thankful to be driving away from the O2, our hands touching but not yet holding.

We pulled up outside her apartment building twenty minutes later. Anita paid, saying that she'd claim it back on expenses. I followed her into the building and up the stairs. She lived in a two bedroom flat on the third floor of a converted block. Upon entering and seeing the high vaulted ceilings and polished hardwood floors, she mentioned that her father had bought the flat years ago, but she paid rent just like anyone else. We took off our shoes and went into the living room, the open curtains letting in the reflected silver glints of light from the Thames. I walked over to the window, while she turned on a lamp, pointing its light to the floor. It was still dark enough in the room for anything to happen.

I looked out – the surface of the water was dark blue and silver, and in constant movement, to the left I could see steam rising from the blinking tip of Canary Wharf.

'You can go out if you want. There's a balcony,' Anita said, her beauty beginning to emerge.

I shook my head, 'Inside's just fine.'

I took a seat while she went to the kitchen, coming back with two wine glasses and a bottle of wine.

'I hope red's OK, it's all I've got.'

I poured the wine while she put a CD on. It was the soundtrack to *In the Mood for Love*, weeks later we would watch the film and I would understand why she chose it, the anguish and uncertainty of sharing a cab ride home with someone you knew you could love clearly resounding in her mind.

'Tell me about your life,' she said, sitting next to me.

'What do you want to know?' I asked.

'Anything, whatever you want to tell me.'

I knew it was one of those crossroads questions, Anita's playful and childlike nature returning. I took a long sip of wine to buy me some more time.

'Well, I went to Cambridge, studied History of Art. Now I work with photographs but would love to work in a museum or something like that. I've been in love once, quite possibly twice. I have had, however, many, many lovers.'

She touched my arm with her index finger, prodding me, almost as if to check that I was real.

'Nice try,' she said, reaching for a remote control. She skipped the music ahead to a track called 'Quizàs, Quizàs, Quizàs', sung by Nat King Cole. She took my hand. 'Do you dance?'

I didn't want to say no. 'Yeah sure, but you lead.'

We stood and moved nearer to the window. I took off my blazer. Anita held both my hands, guided by the light in her eyes, and the soft whispers of her voice, we danced, slightly off beat, accepting that the tempo was too fast for our tired and tipsy feet, our bodies drawing closer and closer from verse to verse. Before long our bodies were perfectly aligned. The track ended, our dance became a serene shuffle, our eyes closed, the warmth building between us, not wanting to ruin it with words.

We made our way to the bedroom. I started to unbutton my shirt. Anita asked me to turn around, I heard as she unbuttoned her dress. I took off my shirt and trousers.

'Can I turn around?' I asked.

She said yes. She had changed into pyjamas, the shape of her body lost in the loose-fitting cotton.

'We're just going to sleep right? I can trust you on that?' she asked.

I told her she could trust me. We got into bed, both of us laying on our backs staring up at the ceiling, not quite sure what to do.

'We haven't brushed our teeth,' she said, an air of domesticity settling in between us.

'Not quite the oral event I was thinking of,' I said, regretting it until she laughed and rolled on top of me. I could feel the pressure of her pubis meeting with mine, the tip of her breasts touching my chest.

'Close your mouth, keep your lips pressed together,' she ordered softly.

I did as she asked, she did the same, leaning in and kissing me, rather like two children forced to kiss each other at a party. I felt the small of her back, she felt the swelling of my penis, our eyes fixed, our lives already entwined.

As the evening progressed, I became increasingly fixated upon the industrial, wrought iron chain dangling from the ceiling. I pictured myself hanging from it, not quite dead but definitely punished, a spectacle for all to see. I was so distracted Anita looked over her shoulder, half expecting me to be staring at an attractive woman. Instead she saw nothing but the remains of Wapping's former hydraulic power station, now a trend setting restaurant, filled with furniture from Vitra placed among the green silenced turbines, girders and chains.

'What *are* you looking at?' she asked, annoyed that I wasn't paying attention to her words.

'Just the machines. I was wondering if they still work. I doubt no one predicted that this place would one day house people eating truffle mash and gnocchi.'

I looked down at my plate, Anita looked at hers. I had ordered the gnocchi hoping that she would reciprocate and order one of the cheaper dishes, I dry swallowed when she ordered the sirloin steak, and then promptly put half of it on my plate.

She changed the subject, 'I read your photo essay.'

'You did?' I had completely forgotten about it. 'What did you think?'

'I thought it was good. Did you write it yourself?'

I knew she didn't mean it like that, nevertheless she reached her hand out and touched mine.

'I did write it, but I got a few people to read it over and make suggestions.'

'You should write more often. Haven't they given you another piece to do?'

I shook my head, forked a few gnocchi hoping I could fill my mouth with food and never speak again. We were nearing the conversation I had been avoiding for weeks. Anita noted the evasive look in my eyes, chose to eat some steak instead of speaking out. It was something that stemmed from our counselling sessions – different methods to avoid conflict. If she kept silent, she knew I would eventually speak.

'There is something I've been meaning to tell you. About work.' Anita didn't say anything, her eyes had opened wide, I carried on, 'The magazine has gone further down the pan. They've made a few people redundant, and have cut the hours of most of the others.' She still didn't say anything, not even an anxious nod of encouragement. 'Well, luckily I've still got a job, but they've asked me to work a four-day week.'

She touched her chest and sighed, 'Gosh, well I guess it could have been a lot worse. When does that start?'

Now, I could have lied and said January, but I want you to know that there is a big enough difference between lying and keeping something secret. It was time to let that plane land. I moved my plate to the side of the table.

'I've been wanting to talk to you about this for a while. They put me on reduced hours in November.'

She didn't say anything. Her face was like the spinning beach ball on a Mac. I could tell she was trying to review the last six weeks of our lives in her mind's eye.

Her voice was vibrato, 'But if you've not been going to work on Fridays, then where have you been going?'

I had to say something that sounded productive, 'I've been going to the library.'

'The library,' her face had turned crimson. 'What for?'

'To read. And I've been searching for freelance picture research work.'

'Have you got any?'

'Not yet, but I'm working on it. I was hoping to have something lined up to make up for the loss of income, but it's all dried up. I wouldn't be surprised if some places were using Google Images to do their picture research work.'

She didn't laugh, she was doing her best not to sound shrill, 'But you've been dressing for work every Friday. You said you had a work event yesterday, why would you go to a work event if you weren't at work?'

She had me there. I couldn't tell her about Rubina, that would have been it. 'I wasn't doing anything.'

'You must have been doing something. You weren't at home. I was sat at home wondering where my fucking husband was.'

Her veneer had cracked, a few of the beautiful people around us looked, eyes filling with tears, her voice dropped to a tight whisper.

'You've been pretending to go to work for weeks. Why would you do something like that? What the hell were you thinking?'

'I didn't want to worry you.'

'You didn't want to worry me. How considerate of you.'

Sarcasm never suited her. She paused expecting me to speak.

'The doctor told me I had to help manage your stress after it happened again.'

'Don't call her 'it'. How dare you.'

I apologised. I didn't like to say her name. Anita pushed her plate away. The food had long gone cold.

'I want you to wait here,' she said, steel in her voice, a vein throbbing on her left temple. 'I'm going home to pack a few things, then I'm taking the car and going to my parents'.'

I reached out to touch her hands, she pulled them away.

'Don't do that,' I said. 'I know I'm in the wrong. But it happened. I didn't know how to deal with it. We've had nothing but bad news this year. Don't go to your parents. Not over this.'

The levee finally broke. Anita wiped the tears away with her sleeve.

'It's not just this . . .'

She trailed off as she got up and walked to one of the waitresses, asking for her coat as she headed towards the exit, the eyes in the room following her out and then returning to stare at me.

THE HOUR BEFORE DAWN

I took off my tie and unbuckled my belt. I tried to remember the last time I wore a suit. I think it was actually at a funeral. The memory of a troubling day spent driving around east London, the grey skies matched by the ashen expression on my dead great uncle's face, eyes closed, mouth filled with flowers and ceremonial sweatmeats. That was a bad day, put in perspective it towered over my trip to Chancery Lane to meet with a recruitment consultant. He was a well oiled, swarthy man in his late twenties. He read through my CV slowly like he was committing it to memory, only looking up to say, 'Bit of a comedown, eh?'

I sat back and stared at him, mentioning that times were tough. He nodded and said that I wasn't alone. With Anita staying with her parents, I had spent the best part of five days trying to get some sort of work to fill my Fridays. I exhausted all the ins I had with picture libraries, most were sympathetic, a few of my contacts failed to reply, the veiled cry for help leaving a bitter taste. During tough times, you'll often find that you are on your own, but that also means that you're standing on your own two feet. I worked my way down my skill and experience set and ended up in the shared office of the recruitment consultant. A thin smile on his lips, air sucked in when I told him I'd only be available on Fridays. I conceded the occasional Saturday. There was a job working in a call centre in Shoreditch. He'd have to fudge my experience somewhat, but they'd probably take me as they needed more mature people who wouldn't 'dick' them around. I nodded and smiled.

I'd have to take off a morning to have an assessment, any actual work wouldn't start until the New Year. I reassured myself that it still gave me time to find freelance picture research work, or perhaps take on an additional role at the magazine. No matter. I was back home in my wife's flat, secure that I had paid my share of the rent and utilities. Eight days before Christmas, I realised that Anita and I hadn't made plans to spend time with each other's families. It was silently understood that we'd be spending the week apart. It assuaged the feeling of absence and loss. The thought hadn't entered my mind that she wouldn't come back. I sat down on the sofa that faced the living room windows, stared out like I was watching TV. The river was at high tide, the patchwork of lights that spread across Canary Wharf defied the gloom.

It was on a similar grey day that Anita and I agreed to marry. We were sat in the living room, the TV on, volume turned down low to help fill the gaps in conversation. We had been treading the path between friendship and love for several months, both of us under pressure to marry, both of us acknowledging when we had had an arranged meeting. Anita sat close to me on the sofa, her hand lingering on my thigh. We had kissed, slept next to each other, felt each other, but we still had not had sex. I wasn't exactly in a position where I could play the field. I assumed that she felt the same way. She picked up her glass of wine, took a long sip and then sighed. She had seen a prospective match the night before.

'He had an earring.' She leaned back and carried on drinking.

'Is that it? "He had an earring"?'

'What more do I need to say? It was a gold stud. I just sat there staring at it wondering why the hell I'd get married to a guy who wears a gold stud. He also said I had "sweet dimples", she sucked in her cheeks. I touched her chin.

'You do have sweet dimples.' She moved my hand aside. 'What have you told your folks?' I asked.

'Nothing yet. I said I needed more time to think. At this stage they know what that means. They get disappointed, throw a guilt trip, try to talk me round, then accept. It's like some sort of twelve-step process. I just don't get why they keep introducing me to such drongos.' She paused to drink some wine, her eyes flashing like two bulbs. 'I just wish they would introduce me to someone like you.'

'"Someone like me"?' Blood ran to my cheeks, she looked out to the river. I shifted in my seat. I expect we had been both thinking the same things, but weren't quite sure who'd be the first to bring it up.

'You know what I mean. Not someone like you. Just you. You know what my parents are like about status.'

By status she meant me being a chamaar. An untouchable. I didn't want to talk about it. I got up and put my glass on the coffee table. Feeling that hollow feeling in your stomach, when the one you love squeezes your heart unnecessarily, I said I needed to get back to my flat in Stepney. I put my coat on, had my hand on the front door handle. She had followed me out of the living room.

'Don't go,' she said in a constricted whisper. I turned to face her. 'It was a silly thing to say. I do want to marry you Tarsem.'

'You do want to marry me?'

'Yes,' she said in a tone that inferred a 'but'.

Feeling that I would break the momentum we had created by taking off my coat and staying, I pulled the handle down and opened the door.

'Fine. Let's get married then.'

I got up and put on a Bill Withers record, his booming, melancholic voice on 'Hope She'll Be Happier' filling the room. I dialled Anita's mobile fully knowing that she'd put me through to voicemail. I heard the ring, the redirection not having the same effect on me anymore. I had no idea what I would say.

'Anita, I saw about some work this morning. I'll probably be starting working Fridays and some weekends in the New Year. At least that's something. Anyway, this has gone on long enough. I'll come up to Harrow tomorrow morning. I hope we can talk.' I hung up.

I left my mobile on the coffee table and went to the bedroom to change. I heard the familiar beep. I hoped it was her. Instead it was a text message from Rubina:

Hey, talk on at the frontline club tonight at 7, got a spare ticket. Wanna join me? Ruby x

I felt a familiar rush of emotion, that feeling of something new, of love lost and found, and the dread that it would to lead to everything turning horribly wrong.

Rubina and I took our seats near the back of the room.

I had known about the Frontline Club for quite a while – usually in connection with a particular reportage photographer – but had never made the trip to Paddington. Rubina seemed to be a regular, a few people grabbed her on our way in, air kissing while eyeing me suspiciously. They were older Asian men, artsy but haggard, they broke the perception I had that British Asian men were either my age or my father's age and there was nothing in between. Clearly there was. Introductions were kept short and forgotten as soon as they passed. The information I took to my seat was that each of them wanted Rubina, and that I was filling in for someone they knew quite well.

The talk was about the use of social media as a means of new journalism in the Middle East. The panel was a mixture of journalists and exiled bloggers mostly from Libya, Iran and Egypt. I drifted in and out of the conversation. In no small way social media was killing my professional career, firstly as more and more emphasis was being placed on keeping up with developments in real time, secondly as the lines had blurred between professional and amateur photography and how I was required to source images. Between my inward facing sulks I heard how – in one way or another – people were changing the world around them. It wasn't even a slow change, it was fast, faster than governments could handle.

Rubina listened to the panel's words as if she were committing them to memory. I stole glances by pretending to look at the photographs hanging on the walls. Her hijab was a navy blue embroidered with gold thread. She was wearing foundation, her large mahogany eyes framed by mascara, lips moist and delicately pursed as she listened. She looked at me through the corner of her eyes, her hand changed position on her knee like she was about to touch me but then changed her mind. I moved my knee to touch hers, she didn't react, eyes refocussing on the panel, a thin smile on her lips.

After the talk, we moved downstairs to the Club's bar. Being one of the first ones down we were able to grab a small table near a window that overlooked the grubby chaos of Paddington below. I ordered two cranberry juices, glanced around the room as it filled. Without alcohol my mind was too clear. I thought ahead, got as far as the next day when I would take the train up to Harrow and beg for Anita to come back home with me.

But there I was with the other woman I had loved. The movement between the two blurring between past, present and future.

I took my seat. Rubina was playing with a bit of tinsel that lined the window sill.

'They've really gone to town with the decorations,' she said, clinking my glass.

'Been a shit year for everyone. At work they put up a plastic tree from Argos in the reception, until one of the directors stumped up the cash for something a little less crappy.'

'How's it going?'

'It's going, that's as much as I can say.'

Rubina looked to the street below. It was a week before Christmas and I was bringing her down. I straightened my back and forced a smile.

'You were really into that talk.'

'Those men and women are an inspiration. The way they've put their lives at risk. The way they've been fighting against dictators who are only in power because the stranglehold they have on their country's natural resources,' she looked at me directly, a mischievous look in her eyes that reminded me of our Cambridge days when we used words like 'sophistry' and 'deictic'. 'I take it you weren't so convinced.'

'You want to know what I honestly think?' I said.

She nodded like it was a question I shouldn't need to ask.

'Well, it bugs me that some blogger sitting in his comfy chair tapping away moans about his governments is being treated like he's the new Che Guevara.'

'There's more to it than that.'

'Ok, granted they give an untainted insider view, but they are also biased. Just the other way.'

'But the work they are doing is helping to bring real change. For decades these governments have had the tightest of grips on the media, social media has blown that away.'

'I'm changing my Facebook status to "Revolutionary."'

'Don't scoff. I bet you've never been on a protest.'

She had me there. I shook my head, my bravado beginning to shrink.

'Not even the march on Iraq?'

I reached my hands out and opened my palms.

'Well, did it stop the war?'

She smacked my hands away playfully.

'That's the sort of cowardly shit that non protesters come out with. Believe it or not but those people who marched on Whitehall did make a difference,' she drank some of her juice. 'Surely this so called "Age of Austerity" must have incensed you in some sort of way. I didn't take you to be the spineless type.'

I stiffened, playing into her game, 'I'm not. I mean there is actually something I'd go out and protest about.'

'What?' Rubina said, leaning forward, the light from the streetlights outside framing the glint in her eyes. 'Go on.'

'I am pissed off about the plans to close down libraries.'

'Libraries!'

'Hey, you can't big up the bloggers without accepting that libraries are a crucial part of our civilisation.'

'Civilisation?'

'Well maybe not in such grandiose terms, but if we lose our libraries we lose opportunities for social mobility, we lose the battle against illiteracy, we lose focal points for our communities to come together.'

'Well,' she said while clinking my glass, 'it's nice to hear you wax so eloquently about something. Reminds me of the old days.'

In the old days we would drink and chat endlessly about things we were studying and the constant trumpeting of our working class roots. It was a genre of conversation that never seemed to go anywhere, perhaps because we were both waiting for the other to make a move. I didn't want to walk the same circle.

'Ok,' I said, moving my glass closer to hers, 'with all the closures planned, I'm sure there will be a protest somewhere. If I go to one, will you come with me?'

'If it breaks your protest virginity, then sure.'

'"Protest virginity?"'

The word reminded me of what I was doing, or at least angling to do. Rubina was thinking too, I saw her cheeks go red. Since we were both thinking about something vaguely related to sex, I thought I could be forthright:

'Are you going out with someone?'

She looked stunned, 'Why do you ask?'

A question answered with a question is surest route to nowhere.

'No particular reason. I was just wondering since you had a spare ticket for this event . . . ' My voice trailed off. Rubina looked at me like a lawyer cross examining a witness. The levity and light suddenly sucked out of the conversation.

'Well if you must know, I was supposed to go with a work friend, but she called in sick today,' she put extra emphasis on the word 'she'.

I looked to the street below for inspiration.

'I don't mean to pry. I just wanted to find out a bit more about you.'

'You will,' she said offering a facile smile.

She got up and said she needed to go to the loo. I watched her disappear into the crowd. Looking back down to the street, the revellers and the lovers crisscrossing with the lonely and the meek, I felt my first pang of danger and guilt. And for the first time that evening, I wondered if it was worth begging Anita to come back.

I got off the train at Harrow-on-the-Hill and made the short walk to Anita's parents' house. Our car wasn't in the drive, neither was her dad's. I stood before the imposing Edwardian semi-detached house, my breath a plume of white escaping before me. It wasn't the kind of weather to be stuck outside with nowhere to go. I saw a twitch of curtain lace in the front room window. I expected it would be Anita's mother. Now that I had been spotted, I couldn't exactly turn back and head back to the station. I made the slow approach to the house, the drive still coated with morning frost.

I rang the doorbell, an old fashioned ringer sounded, the kind that made you picture a tiny hammer and bell. Even though she had spotted me, I was sure that she would stand on ceremony and pretend that my arrival was some sort of unpleasant surprise. She was a former school administrator, a prolonged period of depression putting an early end to her career. She had however retained the supercilious, patronising tone of someone who worked with children.

'I'm glad you came so soon,' she said, having opened the door to a crack like I was a door-to-door salesman.

'Can I come in please?'

'She's not here. You should have come earlier.'

'I know, but I'm here and it's freezing outside. Can I at least come in to warm up?'

She tilted her head ever so slightly and opened the door wide enough for me to come in. I took off my coat and shoes and followed her into the living room, gravitated towards the roaring gas fire until she instructed me to sit down.

'I was going to make chai. You want English tea?'

I nodded. I saw a glimmer of sympathy in her eyes, extinguished as she blinked and left the room. I got back up and stood by the fire. I had only been to Anita's house a few times. The uproar caused by our union – pretty much on both sides – put pay to parental visits as part of married life. Their five-bedroom house was a clear statement of wealth, which eclipsed my parents' humble three-bed home. Anita's father started out as a labourer, he invested a modest inheritance in property, which grew from year to year, through boom and bust. I had never asked but I guessed that he was a millionaire. This was another obstacle that sprouted like an onyx obelisk the moment we became engaged. To love a rich woman is one thing, to marry her, completely another.

Anita was the youngest of four and the only one to have a 'love' marriage. The others were married with kids and living elsewhere in suburban London. It was clear that she was her parents' favourite, the childhood photographs of her outnumbering that of her siblings by quite some margin. I picked up one from the mantlepiece. She was six or seven, her black hair in pigtails, her cherubic face exhibiting the dimples that would deepen as her face matured. She had inherited them from her father, her mother's face was narrow and severe. As my wife went through various diets, and the stress and depression of losing two children, she had lost a lot of weight. I could see the resemblance to her mother emerging. Some people were sunrise, some were sunset. I knew that Anita would eventually be both.

Her mother came back in the room with the cups of tea, obligatory over filled bowl of sugar and small plate of biscuits on a tray. I put the photograph back carefully and sat down, she took the things off the tray, took it back to the kitchen, then sat next to me. She prompted me to drink.

'You don't have to be polite with me,' she said, taking a digestive and breaking it in two. 'What have you been playing at?' When I didn't answer she said, 'Being a husband is about talking to your wife. Talking about everything. Are you cheating on her?'

'Cheating on her?! Where did that come from?'

'Are you?'

'No. Is that what Anita thinks?'

'It's one of the things she's worried about. How can you expect her to trust you when you've been lying to her about your work?'

'I know I was wrong not to tell her straight away. The longer I left it, the harder it became. You can understand that at least?'

She didn't answer. Instead she sipped some more tea and told me to eat a biscuit.

'Is it because she earns more money than you?'

I didn't answer. It wasn't the first time that she had mentioned my salary. It was bad enough going through the forensic dissection of my finances when we were engaged, and then the follow up digs disguised as questions.

'When is she coming back?'

'She didn't say. You can't wait here. I don't think that would be a good idea.'

'I told Anita that I was going to come. You say I need to talk to her, but what can I do if she doesn't return my phone calls and disappears when she knows I'm coming.'

A pause then she said, 'I think you should go back to couple's counselling.'

There it was. I knew that Anita's mother had gone through some sort of therapy to help her with her depression. Anita had been sketchy with the details, which was understandable. I sometimes wondered if she had also received some help, having seen her shift from her happy, personable self to dark silence. There was still so much I didn't know about her. Deep down I resented the idea that two people needed to sit in a room with a stranger to air their grievances, and gain a better understanding of each other. If I was honest, which I should be to you if no one else, then I guess there are things that I wouldn't want to tell my wife, let alone a counsellor.

I dismissed the suggestion with a lowering of my eyelids. The cold in my bones now replaced by the heat of shame and frustration.

'I'm planning to go to India for a trip,' I blurted.

Anita's mother raised her eyebrows. She certainly wasn't expecting that. 'What for?' she asked.

'A holiday. My father is going to start building his house. He's going out in February, I want to go and join him for a couple of weeks, and I want Anita to come with me.'

'What did she say?'

I grimaced, 'I haven't asked her yet. I was going to tell her today.' I finished my tea, inwardly pleased that I had at least told someone.

'I don't think it's a good idea. You should be concentrating on your work and your marriage, not going on holiday.'

I wasn't going to argue it with her, I'd save that for Anita. I finished my tea.

'Please tell Anita that I was here and that I want her to come back to Wapping. I'll telephone her later this evening.'

Anita's mother remained silent. I could practically see the cogs turning in her head, the words she planned to tell my wife grinding together. I put on my coat and shoes and left the house, the cold biting instantly. If I could have gone to India there and then I would have without any hesitation. I would have left the words 'work' and 'marriage' far behind me.

Christmas has never been the easiest time for myself or my parents. In my youth they would spend most of the time visiting relatives with boxes of chocolate for their children. Years later they were doing the same, only handing over the chocolates to the children of the children they had watched grow up, marry and move on in their lives.

Feeling vulnerable and childlike, I had been left alone in the house in Hornchurch on Christmas Eve. My parents were only a few streets away. I didn't want to go with them and be reminded of the things I didn't have. And I didn't want to see the pained expression on their faces as they played with someone else's grandchildren. It was bad enough when I was single and then, when I got married, watching their expectations implode when Anita had her first miscarriage. The past is the past, my father told me, but home always seemed to be the place where bad memories and misadventures would collect like the dispossessed at a shelter, not sure where else they could go.

I sat on the floor in my bedroom going through boxes of old photographs from my university days. I told myself I was looking to collect a few of the best ones, so I could take them to Wapping and scan them, really I was just looking for photos of Rubina. It had been a strange night at the Frontline Club. Not enough of a date to be adulterous, but more than enough awkwardness and unease to make it clear that we were both thinking about the same thing. I searched through the box and found only one photograph of her. It was deliberate, both of us careful not to be caught in any photographs that would lead to questions and inquisitions, especially in the early days.

I remember taking the photograph. It was near the end of our first year. We had finished our finals, a group of us sitting on the Backs near the river Cam, a ratio of 3:1 of beer cans to people, some of us upright, some lying on the grass staring up, seeing no distinction between the sky and their future. I had my now antique Nikon SLR, originally with hopes to become a photographer, or at least get a few snaps in *Varsity*. I waited until her boyfriend, a white guy named Steve, moved away to take a phone call, then I took my snap, Rubina made a self-conscious yelp. I think she was just worried that she'd been photographed with cans of beer, but more so she was annoyed I hadn't given her a second to prepare for the shot.

I actually only saw the photograph a few months later, when I finally developed the film, another thing completely lost in the digital age. Rubina was wearing a beautiful cotton dress, the fabric bearing red and yellow flowers like a landscape painted by Georges Seurat. She sat on the grass with her thin, smooth legs outstretched, her arms propping her up, the deep cut of her dress revealing an ample cleavage. Her black hair was in thick, soft curls, the lightest application of lipstick and eyeshadow accentuating her natural beauty. In that split second, I had caught her face in an expression free from dissimulation, her mahogany eyes revealing a pain, a hint of sorrow from her to me.

From what I remember, Steve was a natural scientist with not much going for him except the Polo Golf he kept parked out near the Grafton Centre. We hardly talked. He knew me as the guy who was close to Rubina in Michelmas term, but, for some reason, hadn't quite managed to sleep with her, or do anything else for that matter. Opening the box released those memories. I held the photograph with one hand, hovering the other hand to cover her hair.

Rubina had sent me a text a day or so before – fairly generic, wishing me a merry Christmas and hoping that we meet up soon in the New Year. She signed off the text with three kisses. Like a hormone-ridden teenager, three kisses from a beautiful woman to an unhappily married man was something special. It gave me hope. It was clear that she needed me as much as I needed her. And while things were ambiguous, we could pretend that we weren't hurting anyone. I put the photograph back in its place underneath a stack of photographs. I hadn't replied to Rubina's text. I needed more time to decide what to write.

I put the boxes away and went downstairs to the living room. The sun was setting, the sky set aflame, a new frost setting across the lawn. I turned on the fire, feeling the force of a cold that never really affected the flat in Wapping. I picked up my mobile. I was thinking of Anita. She'd be eating with her family, playing with her nephews and nieces, watching TV. I was hoping her time away was coming to an end, that 2011 would be a fresh start for both of us. I dialed her number expecting it would go through to voicemail. To my surprise, she answered after the third ring.

'Hi Tarsem,' she said, 'Merry Christmas.'

'Merry Christmas. How have you been?'

'So so I guess. I hate catching the train into work. I have a cold that doesn't seem to want to go away. You?'

'Not much better. I'm in Hornchurch, home alone. I got some work to fill my Fridays. It's nothing special but it will help fill the loss of income.'

'That's good. I'm glad.'

'Did your mother tell you about India?'

She drew in her breath, 'Yes, she told me. I wish I had heard it from you first.'

'I'm sorry. I came to Harrow to talk to you, to tell you. I thought it would be best to tell your mother at least.'

'It's not really the best time to be going on holiday.'

'I know but it's about my dad. I think he wants to retire to India and wanted to spend some time with me while he's sorting things out. I haven't been for years. And you know it might be good for us to get away and spend time in a different environment?'

I knew exactly what she would say.

'I think we need to focus on each other and try to resolve some of the issues we've been having.'

'I agree.'

She paused, expecting me to say more. 'To that end, I think the next step is for me to come back to Wapping.'

'That's great—'

'Let me finish. I think the next step is for me to come back to Wapping on the basis that we'll start couple's counselling again.'

'Oh.' I kept silent. I didn't want to sour the conversation, we had been over my misgivings about therapy enough times. I had to say something positive, 'I understand. I'm willing to try.'

'Good. Let's just start there and see.'

'And India? I don't mean to push, but my dad needs to book the ticket.'

It was her turn to pause. 'Like I said, it's too soon for me, but that doesn't mean you can't go on your own. I doubt your parents want me to come anyway.'

The sentence barbed me, but it wasn't far from the truth. I didn't try to persuade her otherwise. Anita carried on:

'I'll be driving back to Wapping on the second of January. Will you be there?'

'Of course. I can't wait to go back home.'

'Me too.'

'Good. I love you,' I said, it had been a long time since I said those three words.

'Take care,' her voice trailed off. She hung up.

I put my mobile down and looked back to the setting sun. My wife was coming home. It was the news I had been waiting for, but I still felt an emptiness inside. I heard the door open and my parents talking in Punjabi. I sat down and waited for them to come. Dad was the first one to join me.

'You look like you've seen a ghost,' he said, squeezing my shoulder. He was in a good mood, the smell of whisky on his breath.

'I was on the phone to Anita. She's coming back to Wapping.'

'That's good. So, why are you sad?'

'I told her about India. She doesn't want to go, but I do.'

He composed himself. He had asked me several times if I was going to come.

'Are you sure son?'

'Yes. Book me a ticket. Let's do it.'

A smile spread across his face. He wrapped his arms around me and told me he'd book it on Boxing Day. I held onto him and wished that we were already there.

The headline read:

WHITE GIRLS "EASY MEAT" FOR PAKISTANI MEN

The accompanying photographs were mugshots of two Asian men jailed for a string of offences, including rape. I put the newspaper in the bin and looked around the room. I remembered some photographs I sourced for a piece on industrial Britain, sepia-tinted prints of the masses, young men and women covered in dust and grease, standing on the factory line, staring glass-eyed into the lens. The picture I saw wasn't so far removed: an expanse of grey floors and white fluorescent light, people as young as seventeen and old as sixty, most of them seated, some standing, the umbilical cord of their headsets giving them a few feet of walking space, the ringing sound of the automatic dialer sending out a string of warnings.

I had put my dialer on pause. I had lost track of how many calls I had made, my throat was hoarse. Just past the threshold of minimum wage, I hadn't worked this hard in years. The Asian teenager sitting next to me put his dialer on pause.

'Brov, Aidan will be over here if you stay in pause too long,' he said in a benevolent tone of voice. He was one of the top ranking sales people.

Aidan was one of the supervisors, waspish, he would weave from aisle to aisle making sure everyone was working.

I cleared my throat, 'I don't know how you do this. I'm knackered and it's only six.'

'You get used to it. Suck it up like it's spaghetti is what I say.'

He smiled and unpaused his dialer, the familiar beep coming a few seconds later. I knew he didn't want to stay on pause for too long, as that would affect his performance stats. I took a deep breath, sipped some water and unpaused my dialer.

I was selling subscriptions to a newspaper I hated. You'll find that life has a cruel sense of humour, the best thing you can do is laugh about it and not let it pull you under. I wasn't quite at the stage where I could laugh though. In typical fashion I turned up expecting to work on one campaign and was allocated a completely different one. I took it like a bitter pill, leafed through the paper but couldn't really absorb much after reading the front page. I hadn't made any sales, which wasn't a problem as it was my first day and I was only expected to get used to the system. I finished at eight, treaded the icy pavements and caught the East London Line to Wapping.

Rubina had got me thinking about the nature of protest. In the few sales conversations I had, several of the people bemoaned the state of the nation, a few saying that in their day they just put up with it. Putting up with it had become part of the problem, as too many of us – myself included – weren't even able to contemplate change, let alone effect it. The newspaper headline weighed heavy on my mind. It was just like a politician to use words that the press would cling to, string and twist to make the thinnest of stories. The vocal minority misrepresenting the silent majority.

I had sent Rubina a non-committal text saying it would be good to meet up in mid January. She didn't reply. I hadn't told her that I was going to India at the start of February. On the seesaw of life, I felt her drift away as Anita came closer. I had gone back to Wapping a few days early to prepare the flat for her arrival. She arrived on the second of January, inspecting the property like she was a prospective buyer, saying the bare minimum, I knew that she wanted to speak, but was just taking things one step at a time. I prepared dinner while she unpacked. We ate in silence then she said:

'For the time being I think it best if you sleep in the spare room.'

I nodded reluctantly.

'I'm going to give it a week, then contact Kevin Bishop.'

Bishop was the counsellor I found after Anita's first miscarriage. At the time I really had no idea what to do and used the *Yellow Pages* to find someone. I regretted my decision almost instantly. He had a calming voice, but he was overweight and carried a smugness in his eyes. We had some counselling as a couple, and some on an individual basis. I really didn't like the idea of him spending time alone with my wife.

I drank some water before speaking. 'I'm all for going back to counselling but could we try someone other than that guy. I get a bad vibe from him.'

Anita paused as well. It was like we were both getting our words signed off before we spoke them. 'Kevin knows our case history, it would make most sense to use him again, rather than go through sessions with someone new. Don't you think?'

The underlying statement was that he'd be cheaper, she knew I wouldn't argue with that. I nodded again. 'Is there anything else?'

'Yes,' she looked me in the eye, she had lost more weight, which made her brown eyes look bigger. 'I just wanted to say that I understand that you're going to go to India, but also that you have to accept that it's coming at the worst time.'

The statement hurt, and reflecting on it as I walked home, I understood that protest didn't have to be a person shouting, stomping, or waving fists. All it had to be was a person saying what they truly felt inside to the person who needed to act, who needed to change. I blinked acceptance. There was no point in explaining it. The way we spoke was matter of fact, it couldn't lead to an argument. That was a week ago, things had been slowly improving since then.

I let myself into the flat. I could hear Anita pottering about. She came to the hall to greet me.

'So how was it?' she asked.

'Terrible.'

I told her the campaign I was working on, her jaw literally dropped.

She touched my arm. I couldn't be 100% sure, but I think it was the first time she had touched me that year.

'That's shitty. I would have walked out after ten minutes.'

'I thought about it, but you know there was a strange warmth about the people working there. Most were young, Asian and black, a few of them with the usual attitude, a lot of them were genuinely nice, a far cry from the sniffiness I get at the magazine.'

'Right. Well, that's good.'

She was humouring me, but it didn't matter. I took off my coat and shoes.

'I made kim mar,' she said.

Anita rarely cooked Indian food – it was a sign that she was trying to make things work. I had to reciprocate. 'Why don't you go and get changed, I'll serve up.'

'Sure,' I said.

Instinctively I leaned in to kiss her, the move taking her by surprise, her lips aeroplaning away, so my lips brushed against her right cheek. She held me by both arms, I didn't move, neither did she, we could taste each other's breath, the familiar scent of her perfume taking me back a few years.

'I need to check the food,' she whispered, both eyes closed. She let go and turned and walked back towards the kitchen.

Rubina emailed me to say that there was going to be a national protest against library closures, she suggested we attend the event at her local library in Crouch End on that Saturday. It was a week before I was due to leave for India. I mulled it over. I had told her that it was the only protest I'd consider going to, but considering that things had been improving with Anita, and that we'd be going near her flat, the warnings were clearly there. Such it is with the nature of weakness that the consequences hit you first, but you find the strength to ignore them. I wrote back to her saying that I'd be there.

I spent most of my Friday at the call centre trying to come up with a credible excuse to give to Anita. I had been trying hard, my wife had gone ahead and booked a session with Kevin Bishop without asking me, I didn't argue. We went along and I listened. I was to try to spend at least thirty minutes a day just talking to her about what I was doing, and whatever was on my mind. She was to do the same. And of course we both ignored the advice, I couldn't tell her about Rubina, or the embarrassment of my work situation, or even the pain I felt following the miscarriages. Anita was the same, our conversations stilted and tentative, we may as well have spent the time talking about the weather.

I got home around nine pm, Anita wasn't there. I remembered that she had a launch party to attend, which was bound to run late. I made myself a sandwich and went to bed early, strangely feeling good that any lie had been postponed until the morning.

I reached out for her in the morning light, felt panicked that she wasn't there before realising that I was sleeping in the spare bedroom. There had been no intimacy between us since she came back, in typical fashion it was affecting me more than it was her. It hadn't been discussed in our counselling, I doubted she would bring it up. Her door was firmly closed. I didn't see the need to wake her. I showered and ate, then scribbled her a note that I was going to watch a football match with a friend in north London, and that I'd be back after three.

I took the train from Wapping station and changed at Highbury & Islington. My mind was numb – I'm sure that you understand I find it difficult telling you about this – I was trying my best not to think about actions or consequences. It was a protest in a library, not a secret weekend retreat. But, from what experience I had, the choice of location could not be ignored.

Rubina was waiting for me by the Crouch End exit to Harringay station. It was late January, the pavements covered in grit, the sky the colour of snow the day after it has fallen. She was wearing a black coat and a multicoloured scarf, her hijab was a pale blue, a thin line of mascara accentuating her mahogany eyes. She was more beautiful than Anita, I couldn't deny that, but there was more to life than beauty. I waved to her as I approached, kept my distance so we didn't enter the awkwardness of kissing cheeks or not. She raised her hand in reciprocation and tilted her head to her right side.

'The library's just over here,' she said, smiling. 'Are you ready to join the revolution?'

'I am ready as I'll ever be.'

The library was literally steps away from the station. It was an impressive, solid-looking redbrick building, which made me feel that it would stand up to the mettle of any government, outliving them by many generations. There was a steady stream of adults entering the building, many of them carrying children.

The foyer was filled with white and red balloons. We stood behind a couple whose child had run to try and liberate as many balloons as possible. They were painfully apologetic, the wife – white, blonde and immaculately dressed – eyed us up, I could tell she was on the verge of asking where our little one was, she bit her lip and moved on.

'Is this a protest or a creche?' Rubina commented as we entered the main room. Chairs had been set up in a semi-circle to focus on an author who was looking through his notes, there was a table with crisps and other snacks, which were quickly being devoured, plus another table with books on sale to help fund improvements in the library. A photographer weaved between the different pockets of people, stopping to take a shot then moving on. I deliberately sat in the furthest corner of the room, hoping that we wouldn't be photographed.

Rubina leaned into me, 'It's not really a protest if you're sitting down comfortably.'

'What do you want us to do? Climb the bookshelves and trash the place?'

She pulled a face, 'I'm just saying that if we were really protesting we'd be sat outside the council or walking down Whitehall.'

I took a deep breath and thought better of speaking. I didn't want to get drawn into a conversation about the nature of protest, especially as I had never really been on one. Instead I leaned across to the nearest shelf and pulled out a book of paintings by Matisse.

'This is why we need to save our libraries,' I said, opening the book to a painting called 'Study of a Nude'.

Rubina leaned across again, the side of her left breast pressed against my arm, she raised an eyebrow, her comment silenced by the call to attention from the matronly librarian at the front of the room. I put the book back in its place, it becoming more apparent that things had changed between us. A decade ago we could sit and drink and talk endlessly about nothing in particular, but we didn't touch, maybe I was reading too much into it, frustrated as I was, but perhaps it was because we were older and more conscious that so much time had been lost.

The sun was beginning to set as we left the library. It was a completely different visual experience, being high up in the hills of Crouch End, as opposed to the riverside in Wapping. The event had not been what either of us expected, the library was safe from harm, unlike many others. The atmosphere was positive, the author performed some poems for kids, the vast majority of parents borrowed the maximum number of books to show their support. I bought a worn copy of a slim paperback on Impressionism, then realising that I'd have to hide it when I got home, or come up with another excuse. I also got a card from the photographer, he had been snapping away through the reading, I was sure he had caught us. He was an amateur, excited when I name dropped the magazine. I told him I'd take a look at his work, which was true.

Rubina was walking in the opposite direction to Harringay station. I stalled. She only realised when she had crossed the road.

'Oh. Do you have to go?' she asked, a little surprised that I hadn't followed her.

I looked at my watch, it was two thirty. I had made my mind up when I saw her walk away from me.

'No, I don't have to go.' I waited for a car to pass then crossed over.

'I thought we could have a cup of tea at my place. There's something I've been wanting to tell you.'

I nodded, she began to walk.

'I just live around the corner, tiny studio flat I'm afraid, but beautiful views of Ally Pally.'

The pavement narrowed. I let Rubina walk ahead so I could check my mobile. Anita hadn't called or texted me. I turned the phone off and followed her to the front door of a salmon-coloured Victorian terraced house. She pointed to the two small rectangular windows in the roof.

'That's me up there,' she said, unlocking the front door.

Both of us were silent as we walked up the communal staircase to the flat, Rubina walked ahead, both of us beginning to feel nervous. I wondered how many times the act of drinking tea had been betrayed by the folly of consenting adults. Rubina slid her key into the lock. Before she opened the door she asked:

'Are you OK?'

Her tone was ambiguous, but I felt that she wasn't asking about my wellbeing, rather whether I was OK about going inside her flat. I shrugged my shoulders nonsensically and made a sound of acceptance.

The front door opened into the main living space: a wood stripped floor covered at the centre of the room by a rectangular Persian rug, a small two-seater settee with similar sized wooden coffee table, a teak, two-door wardrobe and matching small chest of drawers on top of which Rubina kept a few framed photographs, and a double bed in the corner of the room. One door led to the bathroom, the small kitchen was through an alcove, the slope of the roof intruded the closer you got to the bed, the double windows looked out towards Alexandra Palace.

We took off our coats and shoes. In the waning light, Rubina first turned on a couple of small lamps, the light angled towards the floor, rather like the light bulbs had to be there but weren't allowed to watch.

'How do you take it,' she asked.

I was stunned.

Bemused, she said, 'The tea, stupid.'

'Oh, white no sugar.'

She beckoned me to sit down, at first I sat on the settee, then I got up to look at the photographs on the chest of drawers. There was a couple of her with friends, the biggest one was a family portrait. It must have been taken several years ago, her father sat next to her mother, his face gaunt, a kufi hat covering his bald pate. I turned to look at Rubina, she was staring directly at me, the kettle in her hand.

'Dad wanted us to have a family portrait taken. It was about three months before he died.'

'I'm sorry.'

I stepped away from the photograph and sat back down on the settee. Rubina placed the tea down on the coffee table, went to the bathroom then came back and sat next to me. We were contiguous, neither of us feeling the need to adjust. It was almost like we were both where we wanted to be in life, but not quite.

'I was married,' Rubina said, piercing the silence.

'Married?'

'Madness really. It's funny the stupid things you do for your parents.'

I remained silent, she carried on.

'When my father was sick, he kept going on about how I was the only one of his children who was unmarried, and that he wanted to be sure I was looked after before he you know. He became a little obsessed by it, mum of course said that it was helping him, and when I moved back to Birmingham, I couldn't ignore it, not like I had done for most of my twenties.'

'So what happened?'

'I just caved in and said OK. It was like being caught in some sort of tunnel, being sucked along with no control. Mum and I went to Pakistan. I was married to a man they had arranged back home. Three days later dad died. I wasn't there to be with him. Mum wouldn't say it, but she regrets it as much as I do. My brothers, Mo and Kam, said that he was happy, but he was so delirious when I left, I really couldn't be sure that it had registered.' She paused to drink some tea. 'We came back to Britain for the funeral, then flew back to Pakistan. As soon as we touched down in Karachi, I knew that I had made a terrible mistake. The next two months were spent being cajoled into trying to make it work. The final month trying to pull it apart. A quiet disgrace.'

I placed my left hand on her forearm. 'That sounds terrible. I can't imagine what sort of pressure you must have been under.'

She touched my hand, I tried to make nothing of it, she carried on:

'I came back to Britain and moved straight back to London. It took nearly a year for me to go back to Birmingham. It's not been the same since, but I never expected it would be. So there you go. You can see that my personal life is fraught with complications. But what about you? You don't talk about your wife very much, do you?'

I looked at her face, a smile caught against the edge of a tear in her eye.

'I don't talk about my wife very much,' I repeated quietly. 'I guess there's a reason for that.' Rubina squeezed my hand to get me to talk some more, I was scared by the comfort of her touch. 'Well, it would be hard to say that we have a happy marriage, but I don't know who gets married to be happy. We're Asian, we know that, but there's a reason why, probably a few reasons why.'

'Tell me,' she said in a half whisper.

'Well, firstly I think we got married more as a solution to a problem than because we love each other. My mother's never really forgiven me for marrying a Jat. But there's something deeper, more painful: Anita's had two miscarriages in eighteen months.'

Rubina inhaled, her grip softening but ever present.

'We just can't quite find a way to overcome it,' I continued, 'and I can't find a way to talk about it because I know the pain that I feel can never compare to the pain she feels, but it still hurts. Still hurts.' My voice had cracked.

Rubina shushed me, she wrapped her right arm around me and pulled me closer, my head resting on her shoulder. We were silent for a few minutes, the only sound coming from the street below, passing cars, a train rattling in the distance. Our eyes were closed, the sweet salt of tears on our cheeks, I felt her fingers touch my chin, then push past my ear and through my hair, her lips upon mine, my lips upon hers. Not the kiss of lovers, nor of friends, but two people who had let the years slip by, secretly knowing that there was no way back. My fingers caressed her nape, her tongue touched mine, a murmur of happiness escaping from her lips. It was the sound that broke the moment. We knew it had to end, even if we didn't want it to.

'I better go,' I whispered.

'Stay. I want you to stay so much.'

Her hand moved down and touched my thigh. I held it.

'I have to go,' I said a little louder. 'I don't want to, but I have to.'

I got up and straightened my trousers, walked around the coffee table and put on my shoes. Rubina remained where she sat, eyes fixed ahead of her, not wanting to acknowledge my movements. It was like the light had gone out of her eyes. There was nothing I could say, I put on my coat, my heart heavy on my hand as I opened the door and left.

It was the night before leaving. I had moved most of my clothes to the spare room and was in the process of folding T-shirts and pants to add to my small suitcase. I had no intention to pack much, despite my father's promises, I expected that we would spend most of the time in the old house or strolling around the village visiting relatives. I was OK with that – the mindshifts between the magazine and the call centre, the counselling, the evening with Rubina, the freeze between me and Anita all weighed on my mind and body. I was actually looking forward to spending two weeks in the dust and heat of the village, sleeping late into the morning and drinking small cups of sugar-laden tea. Anita knocked on the door. I hesitated before saying she could come in. This is where we were: I was effectively her lodger.

'How's it going?' she asked, her hand still on the door handle.

'Fine. There's really not that much to pack. I think it's going to be hot.'

'Have you had your injections?'

I shook my head.

'Sem! Make sure you get some mosquito spray, they're going to be all over you.' There was genuine concern in her voice. It made me feel that she still loved me. Love can be that simple, really.

She came and sat down on the bed. I was stood at the foot of the bed. I took my suitcase off the bed and placed it on the floor. I sat down next to her, about an inch or two of space between us.

The tone of her voice changed, 'I'm going to carry on seeing Kevin Bishop while you're away. He did say it was a good idea if we see him individually.'

I remained silent, though I thought Anita could hear the grinding of my teeth. I don't have a problem talking to people. I'm talking to you after all. But it was the idea of paying a stranger good money just to listen, and then ask you the questions you've already asked yourself. Maybe it was because the counsellor was a man, and that in spite of the calmness and neutrality of his face, I occasionally caught him looking at Anita in a way that was unseemly. Anita changed the subject:

'You'll call me when you get there right?'

'Of course.'

'What time will it be?'

'I think I arrive around three in the morning. Here it will be around ten or eleven at night?'

'That's fine,' she said looking down and touching the space between us. 'Even though we're going through a hard time, I just wanted to say that I'm going to miss you and that I'm happy that you'll be spending some time with family.'

I held her hand, she didn't flinch.

'I'm going to miss you too.'

I could tell she was thinking about saying something, instead she released the thought as a sigh. Feeling like the moment was going to pass, I leaned across and kissed her on the cheek. She smiled, the faint rouge of a blush appearing on her cheeks.

'I better let you finish packing. What time are you leaving in the morning?'

'About eight if I'm going to take the Piccadilly line.'

'OK,' she let go of my hand and stood up. 'I'll be able to say "bye" before I go to work.'

She wished me a good night as she closed the door.

I couldn't sleep. I spent the best part of an hour trying to map the different sounds of the flat to see if Anita was still awake. I could hear the creak of the floorboards from her bedroom, I was sure she was pacing around. The sound becoming rhythmical, the rhythm meeting my breathing, as I eventually fell asleep around one or two am. I woke to the sound of footsteps in my room, sitting up I saw Anita stood still before me, like we were playing a game of blind man's bluff and she was just about to be caught. She was wearing the thin cotton nightdress she used to wear when we first married.

'I didn't want to sleep,' she said, still stuck on her feet. 'I've been having the strangest feeling that you won't be coming back.'

'What?' I said wiping the sleep from my eyes. 'I'm sure after a few days with my parents I'll have my bags packed ready to come home.'

In the half light she didn't look convinced.

'Come here,' I uttered, pulling the envelope of the duvet open. The spare bed was a single. It was Anita's old bed from her parents' home. We had never slept together on it. She approached on the balls of her feet, the curves of her body visible through the nightdress. 'It's been so long,' she muttered, the words drifting off like footsteps in the sand, she slipped herself into the bed, aligning her body to face mine. I gave her half of my pillow, our heads still, custodians of each other's eyes.

'I love you,' she said.

'I love you too. I always have,' I replied.

She leaned into me, kissing me as if for the first time, the awkward meeting of teeth as we reacquainted ourselves with each others lips. Anita was a slow, cautious kisser, her tongue only entering my mouth after a minute or so. I placed a tentative hand on her hip, her hand moved down to touch mine, then travelled across to touch my stomach, her fingers pulling on the elastic of my boxers. She pushed her body against mine, her lips moving up to brush against my earlobe.

'I want you inside me,' she whispered.

I moved so I could take off my T-shirt, nearly fell from the edge of the bed. Anita pulled me back, I helped her take off her nightdress. She kissed my chest, then moved down to pull my boxers off. She had never been like this, even when we were on our honeymoon. She held the shaft of my penis, pulling the foreskin back as she placed her lips around the head. I touched her hair, whispered that it was my turn. I pushed her onto her back, let the duvet fall to the floor, her breasts naked before me for the first time in months. I kissed a path down to her navel, she lifted her hips to help me remove her underwear. I kissed her inner thigh, my hands touching her chest, her breathing rising in intensity as I pushed my tongue into her vagina, the tip of my tongue feeling for her clitoris. After only a few seconds she tugged my hair, her legs stretching, I cupped my arms beneath her knees.

'Slowly,' she instructed, her eyes closed, head tipped back, her hand reaching down to guide me in, our breathing unifying as I began to push. Sex can be beautiful, most of the time it is the awkward clashing of two bodies. At Anita's insistence I pushed harder, our movements syncopated, her head banging against the headboard. 'Don't stop,' she muttered, her legs rising, I helped lift them onto my shoulders, sweat beginning to drip from my forehead to her stomach. I watched Anita's body twitch, her forearm covering her eyes, she didn't want to see me as my movement accelerated to its fatiguing conclusion. I put her legs down and flopped beside her, both of us spent and not wanting to say a word.

It was the hour before dawn. The birds beginning to sing through the darkness. I reached across and picked up the duvet and covered our naked bodies. Still silent, Anita turned on her side and lay her head on my shoulder, a kiss gracing my cheek, her right arm holding me in place. The morning would come. There was nothing we could do about it but sleep for two hours, maybe three, hold each other close and kiss, not knowing that the next two weeks would change both our lives.

BETA

The snake of people shook from head to tail, all of us looking back at a pair of women who had started fighting. They had been on a different flight to me, probably had to fly through Turkmenistan or Qatar, making it to the back of the immigration queue adding insult to injury. The line – 90% of them men – cheered at first, a couple of them intervening before things became ugly. Beneath the bright fluorescent lights of Amritsar airport everything was reflected, ceiling to floor and back again endlessly.

I looked out for father, spotted him when I was more advanced in the line, kept waving until he spotted me. He breathed a sigh of relief and waved back. Him and mother had been there for over a week. They were brought up in different villages on the outskirts of Jalandhar. I'd be staying in my grandmother's house on my father's side, though I was sure I'd also have to spend a few days in mother's village too. Because of the sheer volume of things to do and people to meet, my parents usually stayed in their villages. I think they were happy with that arrangement, though they would never admit it.

I made it through immigration without any questions or long stares, felt slightly sheepish to be pulling along my small cabin suitcase. Father hugged me then said:

'Where's your suitcase?'

'This is it. I thought I'd travel light.'

He furrowed his brow. 'But you're going to have to take back presents with you,' then he switched to Punjabi and said that I never think things through.

I told him I was sorry.

'This way, the driver's waiting. Gurjit, do your remember him?'

I shrugged my shoulders. I had vague memories of being driven around in a small camper van, when I was a teenager, but I couldn't remember the driver.

'Well he remembers you,' father said leading the way.

I hadn't reset my watch so I had no idea what time it was, probably around three or four in the morning. Approaching the exit beneath the bright lights only accentuated the darkness outside. The first thing to hit was the change in temperature, it was cold outside, then there was the full spectrum of new odours, finally the buzzing sound of mosquitoes. We negotiated our way around families waiting to leave and taxi drivers and baggage handlers touting for business.

Gurjit was waiting in the car park. He no longer had his camper van, instead it was a box-shaped, Jeep-like-but-not-quite vehicle. He was a short, middle-aged man with a commensurate sized paunch, and wearing a white kurta pyjama. He only spoke in Punjabi. He shook my hand, a genuine smile on his face, then looked down at my feet and said:

'Where's your suitcase?'

Father sat upfront with Gurjit, I had the whole of the back to myself. I couldn't sleep, my brain was too wired with the intake of new experiences. The road was straight, sometimes three lanes wide, sometimes just one. There was a completely different set of semantics for driving, based mostly upon the size of your vehicle and how hard and frequently you beeped the horn. It was a battle with oncoming traffic as much as the other cars, coaches, carts, tractors and bicycles Gurjit tried to overtake – a far cry from the pebbled roads of Wapping and the choke hold of the A13. After the second time I thought we were going to die in a head-on collision, I lay down and closed my eyes, not quite asleep but disconnected enough to relax.

I felt the weight of the dawn on my eyelids. I got up and looked eastwards. The sun was rising with great speed, illuminating a flat landscape of occasional buildings, the horizon dotted with trees and a deep, off-white mist. I took out my old Nikon from my backpack and rolled down the window. I had completely forgotten how to use the manual settings, so I flicked it to automatic, waiting for a moment of stability to take a shot. Father looked back at me, a look of displeasure on his face.

'There'll be plenty of time for photos later,' he said in Punjabi so Gurjit could understand. I put my camera away and rolled the window up, the feeling that I was thirteen again rushing back. We arrived at the village around seven or eight am. In a daze, father led me to the house, which looked like a fairly large series of rectangular boxes painted yellow and terracotta. Mother was waiting outside along with an old woman holding a plate full of sugar. The woman stopped me and fed me a couple of fingerfuls, saying something under her breath.

'Who's that woman?' I asked father as we went inside.

'She's your grandmother,' he replied nonplussed.

I woke up in the spare room, a far remove from the rooms in Wapping and Hornchurch. It was larger, with high ceilings and brightly coloured walls, but also devoid of furniture, just a bed with no headboard and a cast metal locker, the kind of thing that would have been more fitting in the changing room of a factory or a fire station. I stared up at the ceiling, finally feeling exhausted, and watched a gecko or some sort of green lizard walk across and down, escaping through a small gap in the window frame.

Father knocked on the door and then walked in.

'Time to get up and have some breakfast,' he said, turning and walking away. I had the feeling that he was excited that I was there with him, but was doing his best not to show it.

I sat up and rubbed my eyes. I had changed into a T-shirt and jogging bottoms, some thin, leather slippers waiting for me to use. Mother, father, and his mother were sitting outside in the back garden of the house around a circular, marble dining table. Mother handed me a plate and poured me a small cup of tea, as expected it was incredibly sweet in a way that made me think of diabetes but feel comforted all the same.

'The toast is in here,' she said pushing a circular, plastic lunch box towards me. I unscrewed the lid, the bread, which had been wrapped in a green tea towel had been toasted on a tuvah with a smear of ghee. Butter and sugar seeming to be the two main Indian preserves. I took two slices, eating it while trying in to take in the new surroundings. Father passed me a copy of *The Times of India*.

'We stopped on the way to get today's copy,' he said, a new, benevolent tone of voice emerging. It was Saturday 5 February 2011.

I flicked through the paper while nibbling on the toast, my parents and grandmother in full flowing conversation, I didn't want to concentrate to understand what they were saying, it was probably better that way. The articles in the paper were short and to the point, there was an article on David Cameron near the back of the paper on the international news pages. At a security conference he had said that multiculturalism in Britain had failed. The article cited parts where he mentioned Muslim youths, fanaticism, forced marriages pretty much all in the same breath. As a counter to this he spoke about traditional British values.

I shuddered. I was sure it was causing a wave of cynicism and anger across the liberal media, the magazine included. I asked father if the house had internet access. He shook his head and said that I should try to get away from work. I folded the paper and looked at my grandmother, as she had been watching me for most of the meal. She was not that much different from the old Asian women I saw walking around Hornchurch, perhaps her skin was a little darker, the texture rougher, like she had been blasted with sand. There was a hardness about the look she gave me, which reminded me of the look my father gave me when we spoke of children, or lack thereof. More than that I guess my grandmother – I didn't even know her name – was trying to figure me out, like I was an abstract painting hanging on a wall or a sentence scribbled in a foreign language. I sat back and smiled until father told me to go and have a bath.

I remembered bathing in the house quite well. The setup hadn't changed much. There was still a cold and hot water tap connected to a combination boiler, which was connected to a canister of gas by a rubber tube, a plastic stool to sit on and a bucket. The floor had been tiled and angled so water would run to the drain in the centre of the room. I scrubbed my body, and washed my hair, feeling strangely refreshed when I returned to the spare room. Seeming like he was tracking my every movement, father came to see me after a few minutes.

'Get your camera and meet me outside,' he said in a direct but jovial manner.

I joined him outside the house. The sky was a clear blue bereft of clouds. The village had grown from what little I remembered. Our house was on the main road that ran from east to west. It had the best maintained road, and the majority of the small shops, but there were now smaller roads that ran parallel to it. The pavements were yellow and dusty, children running barefoot without a care in the world. Father was wearing a white, short-sleeved shirt, the top three buttons open to reveal the greying hair on his chest, polyester trousers with the machine-set creases and thick leather sandals. He was holding a large rolled up piece of paper. I knew what it would be.

We walked a few metres towards the centre of the village than turned left and walked towards his plot of land. There was a number of different fields that stretched out into the distance. Some of them were being used for farming, others were left unkempt, that was the only way to tell which one was which, there were no posts or fences, just different shades of green and yellow. We walked to his plot, which was easy to identify as the grass had recently been cut, a small group of children playing cricket with a broken bat and tennis ball. We stood at the threshold, as he unfurled the schematics for his house. They seemed clear enough.

'There's going to be three storeys, five bedrooms, three of them with their own bathrooms,' he pointed each room out like we were following a map of his life, the compass points being money, land, marriage and children. I couldn't connect to his dreams. I still don't know why. I had to feign enthusiasm when he told me that it would be the biggest house in the village. He told the kids to scram, catching one of them as they ran away. He gave him a ten rupee note and asked him to take a photograph of us both. The boy was ten or eleven. Reluctantly I turned the camera on, took off the lens cap and handed it to him. The boy didn't want an explanation on how to use it. I stood beside father on his land, to my surprise he wrapped his arm around me the second before the iris of the lens clicked. I expected the photograph would reveal my surprise, but there was no way to tell.

The boy handed me back the camera and ran off to join his friends, who were playing on another field nearby. Father looked at me, tenderness in his eyes.

'One day all of this will be yours,' he said, pulling on a tuft of grass to touch the earth beneath.

After a few days life developed into pretty much the same routine my parents had in Hornchurch, only the TV sat in a different corner of the room. Mother had gone to her village to be with her mother and extended family, I was sat on the gaudy faux-leather sofa with father and grandmother. Both ceiling fans were on full speed, I looked up mesmerised by the spinning blades, thought briefly of *Apocalypse Now*, then returned my focus to the news channel blaring on the chunky cathode ray television. There had been an uprising in Egypt. From what I could gather from the footage and reporter, who spoke too fast for me to keep up, the people had risen to topple their government. Father translated a bit for me, said that there were fears that protests would spread across to the Middle East. I harrumphed inwardly, blushing from my memories of the Frontline Club. The bloggers had actually done something. They had started a revolution.

I kept scratching my ankles. The mosquitos were devouring me from the feet up, the bites forming a network of heat spots, which, when scratched, only released more heat throughout my body. Father told me to stop. Grandmother told me to put some cream on it. She pointed to a cabinet, inside which I suppose some medicine. I said I'd be fine. The world was still moving, but we were sitting still. Father broke the stillness by taking out his Indian mobile phone, barking out instructions to Gurjit no doubt.

'Come on, get changed,' he said. 'We're going to Jalandhar.'

'Why?'

'To get a suit made for you.'

'What for?'

'Your cousin's getting married on Friday. I checked your case, you didn't bring a suit.'

I was about decry his invasion of my privacy, but thought better of it. It was his house, more or less his domain. He had asked for my passport and my wedding ring on my first day there, said it would be better to put it in the safe he kept in his bedroom. I was so tired I didn't argue. Father checking my suitcase didn't seem so out of the ordinary.

The drive to Jalandhar only became complicated when we entered the city. The roads were clogged with all manner of vehicles, each of them trying to maintain their own place on the road. Traffic lights seemed to be a relatively new concept, a rule that could be broken like any other. But somehow it all worked, every piece fitted like some wondrous jigsaw.

Father pointed out a huge hospital, I had thought that it was a Gurdwara.

'Jalandhar is the city of hospitals. Best place to get sick,' he joked in Punjabi so Gurjit could join in. The air conditioning inside the car was keeping him cool, as soon as we stepped outside sweat began to seep out of him like he was bleeding.

We walked down the main bazaar of tailors and fabric merchants, the desperate shop workers, whose main role was to stand outside on the street and cajole people in, spotted us from a mile away. It wasn't just me, it was father too. Our clothes, skin, even the way we ambled along made it clear that we were foreigners who had money. I didn't know what father was looking for, but he pointed out a shop to Gurjit and me.

'How about that one?' he said, not interested in our answers.

The shop was run by an overweight Singh who wore a navy blue turban. He was assisted by a couple of teenagers, one of whom was sent off to get us some mango sodas as soon as it was clear that we were going to buy something. At first the merchant spoke to father, then he looked at me.

'Pick a fabric my friend,' he said in English. He had sly eyes, the kind that were always calculating.

The main wall of the shop was covered in rolls of different cloths. It was an overwhelming number of fabrics. The other teenager assistant helped me out by cutting a few samples, one blue, one beige, one black. I picked one. The feeling of consumerism flooding back, filling my lungs as I puffed out my chest. I looked at the Singh.

'I want a single-breasted suit, no shoulder pads.'

There was a car parked outside the house, when we arrived back. We said our goodbyes to Gurjit, then I followed father round to the back of the house so we could get inside and wash up before meeting them. I asked him who they were.

'Your aunty,' he said without hesitating.

That could have meant anything, but I wasn't going to ask for more information. There had been a string of people visiting the house at all hours for four days. I didn't recognise any of them, but of course, they knew me well enough. The only difference here was that we entered the house from the wrong side, which began to trouble me as I was led to the dining room to meet these people.

There was a husband and wife, plus another woman. I shook the man's hand and waved a 'hello' to the two women, then sat down next to father on the sofa opposing them. From what I could gather they were here for the wedding, they asked a few questions about my life in London, which father answered. One of the young women who lived in one of the neighbouring houses made some tea, which she served with biscuits and a mild balti mix. They drank the tea, but left the food untouched.

The second woman hardly talked, which worried me most. She just sat there nodding along to whatever was said, her gaze often turning to me, a rictus grin on her face. The visit lasted less than half an hour. When they left, I stood in the doorway so father couldn't pass.

'What was that about?'

'Family business,' he replied, the benevolence replaced with a stiffness of manner.

He waited for me to move then walked past, stopping after a few paces.

'You know this is the land you came from. You should be more open to people. This isn't London, not everyone is a stranger who wants to ignore you. These people want to know you, so don't be rude about it.'

'I'm not being rude,' I said, my voice trailing off as he walked away.

I went to my room, grabbed my mobile, and made my ascent to my favourite place in the house: the roof. The box-like house had a large flat roof, which had a small makeshift clothesline, water tank and a bench. You could see across to the edge of the village, the different shaped houses, a clear demarcation between those who were being funded by people abroad and those who were not, a few roads, a couple of small schools and shops, then the fields and the plots of land.

I stood in the middle of the roof, the afternoon sun beating down through a cloudless sky. It wasn't hot enough to affect me, the coldness of the nights were a different matter. I turned on my phone and dialled Anita's number. I had called her briefly when I arrived, the call cut short because of my fatigue. This time I hoped we could talk. The call went straight through to voicemail. I hadn't timed it right – so much of life is about timing – she was probably on the tube or in a meeting. I had a couple of seconds to decide whether to leave a message, the beep prompting me to speak.

'Hi Anita, it's me. Just calling to see how you are. I'm OK. The mosquitos are eating me from the feet up. My father bought this thing to plug in at night, not sure if it makes any difference. Everyone's fine. Just a succession of people to see, have only left the village a couple of times, touched base with both grandmothers. That's about it. I'll try to call again later this week. Bye, bye, love you, bye.'

I hung up and turned the phone off. On the roof of a house a few streets away a young boy was flying a purple kite made with what seemed to be wire and wax paper. Behind him, a crisscrossing of wires hanging lank from the pylons that powered the village. It seemed too much like a metaphor for life. I shook my head and watched the boy dance from one side of the roof to the other with no care or regard to the crushing distance of the world below, nor the deadly trap behind him, his creation, an extension to his hands reaching out and up to the heavens. I sat on the bench and watched him enviously, my feet swollen and hands calloused and wished I could have that sense of reckless abandon.

The brass band arrived in the morning. I was outside the house, walking to father's plot to take a photo of the ceremony to bless the land before the foundation work started. I stopped and turned, when the band started playing, announcing their arrival to the whole street in a cacophony that soon became a vaguely familiar tune from an old Hindi film. There was six of them, dressed in matching red kurta pyjama suits and blue turbans, walking side by side like they were in some sort of Indian brass band version of *Reservoir Dogs*. I had to step onto a grass verge to let them by, the tambourine man winking at me as he passed.

It wasn't hard to spot the bride-to-be's house. A fairly large marquee had been erected near it on a unused piece of land, the house itself covered in a veil of multi-coloured LED lights, turned off in the day but illuminating the night better than the sparse streetlights could. I walked behind the band until they reached the house, changing formation, but still playing the same tune. I had my Nikon, I sneaked in a quick snap before the musicians had time to react.

Father was at the site, talking to what looked like the foreman. He acknowledged my approach with a raise of his eyebrows, then carried on talking, his hands moving to every sentence like he was sculpting his words. The foreman was in his early thirties, short and stocky with extremely dark skin. The two men approached me after a couple of minutes.

'Tarsem, this is Balwant. He's going to be overseeing the building work,' father said in Punjabi.

I shook Balwant's hand, he had bright, intelligent eyes. He asked father if there were any other children. The older man answered with a rueful shake of his head. We were all waiting on the priest from the local Gurdwara. Father wasn't a religious man, but he observed religion like he observed the law, careful to make sure he abided with silence and care. Balwant left us and rejoined his team, who were gathered around a digger, waiting.

'He should be here any minute,' father said anxiously.

I thought about reassuring him, but thought it better to remain quiet and follow him as he walked from the plot to the street, peering down it like he was waiting for a bus.

'That band is giving me a headache,' I muttered to break the silence.

'Get used to it. They're going to be here for two days, maybe more. This is a proper Indian wedding son, I'm sure the groom will be riding in on a horse.'

'I can't wait,' I said sarcastically, annoyed by his emphasis on the 'proper Indian wedding'.

The priest appeared in the distance, even I could recognise him, tall, possibly over six foot, wearing a immaculate navy blue kurta pyjama and a turban, which shared the same yellow colour as sweet rice, his beard was long and white, the fuzziness of the hair making almost seem like candy floss. I bowed my head as he passed, not quite sure of what I should do.

'Is it OK to take a photo of him doing this?' I whispered to father.

'Just do it when he's not looking,' he said, turning to greet him.

—

I had always thought that Indians tended to be quiet and a touch on the passive side. I was wrong. The noise only intensified as we moved from day to night. Mother, father and grandmother went to the Gurdwara for the ceremony, I was allowed to stay at home and read, sleep and scratch the increasing range of my body that had been bitten by mosquitoes. They came to collect me in the evening. I took my camera along. It was clear to the entire village that I was a tourist, I thought I may as well play up to the role.

The marquee was full, the bride and groom and their families sat at a last-supper-like table, on one side of the room near small dance floor, the majority of people sitting around scuffed, circular tables, waiting for their food, teased by the savoury smells emanating from the nearby house. On a makeshift stage an attractive, but slightly overweight, female singer was miming and part dancing a Hindi tune. The band was on a break.

We took our seats at a table near the entrance. Mother told me that the groom was an IT consultant from Ilford, while the bride was from the village. She had studied office management in Jalandhar, and had come top in her class. I nodded, not knowing how to take the information. I soon grew tired of the succession of people who came to our table and asked about me like I wasn't there, my parents stuttering when asked why they didn't have any grandchildren. I grabbed my camera and left the marquee.

The surrounding area was flooded with light, I walked until I was at the edge of darkness, the only things touching me were a cool breeze and the shards from the wall of sound behind me. I looked up at the sky, which was so different from London, clearer, different coloured patches sewn by the stars.

'A penny for your thoughts?' I heard someone say in front of me.

I looked down and saw a young woman dressed in a beautiful turquoise sari, her English impeccable, but her accent unmistakably Indian, that metallic twang to each syllable, like her tongue had been dipped in copper.

Her hair was a thick black, her skin pale and catching what remained of the light from the marquee. Perhaps it had been the endless watching of Indian TV adverts, but she reminded me of Katrina Kaif.

'You don't look like you're with the camera crew?' she said, to hide my inability to respond.

I shook my head, the words finally falling out, 'No, I'm not. I just brought this along. I took some snaps but the camera team gave me dirty looks.'

'Dirty looks?' she said, raising a bemused eyebrow.

'I mean they looked a bit angry so I stopped.'

'You're British?'

'Yes. You're Indian?'

'Yes. I'm Lakshmi.'

'I'm Tarsem.'

She extended her right arm. 'In these situations isn't it customary to shake hands?'

I shook her hand, her skin was soft and warm, a confident strength in her grip. I asked her if she was here for the wedding. She nodded.

'I can only take so much. It's like a cattle market sometimes. Don't you think?'

'Yeah I suppose,' I said. 'I used to avoid weddings when was single, now I'm married I never get invited.'

She clipped in, 'You're married? Where's your ring?'

I looked at my left hand, in the half light she could see that I wore no ring, but not the circle of pale skin it left behind. I told her that my father had wanted to keep it in his safe, she didn't seem convinced.

'Are you here for long?' she asked, the tone of her voice sounding like she was politely trying to wind the conversation up.

'No, just a few days more. I'm not so sure if I'm looking forward to going or not.' She tilted her head, beckoning me to elaborate. 'I mean life here is so much different to life in London, where I'm from. I really don't miss the stress of living in a big city.'

'Well, I hope you come back,' she said, stepping forward, walking so close to me I could smell the scent of her perfume. I watched her walk towards the marquee, the bright lights drawing out her figure, which was slender but with enough movement as she sashayed that it reminded me of Baudelaire's poem, 'Le Beau Navire'. I had never really been entranced by the way a woman walked. Perhaps people in London spent too much of their time dragging their feet or rushing from one place to another.

I watched her disappear, my eyes refocussing to another figure, who was watching me as intently as I had been watching Lakshmi. It was mother. She had a look on her face that I couldn't decipher. I knew that meant trouble.

You must watch a film called *Donnie Brasco*. There's a particular scene near the end when Al Pacino gets called to a meeting. He knows he's in trouble. As he's walking to the front door of his flat he pauses and takes off his watch and his rings, a severe look of resignation in his face. That's how I felt when mother asked me to join her and father to travel to Jalandhar and eat at a hotel restaurant. I accepted with a nod of my head and wished that I hadn't given all my valuables to father to keep in his safe.

Gurjit came around midday, spent a few minutes sitting in the house with us to watch the tail end of a drama about a young woman from a poor background who – by chance – marries into money and all the trials and trappings that come with it. As before, father sat up front with Gurjit, while mother sat opposite me. Her skin had darkened, but her hazel eyes had lightened. She sat still, both hands positioned to keep her steady, she wore a pink silk salwar kameez. It was impossible for me to escape her field of vision, so I opted to stare out the window as the dry fields became houses and the houses became shopping malls and hospitals. Father only looked back at us once, to tell me that we'd be eating at the Taramount Hotel. He was excited, I guessed it might be like eating at the Ritz or the Wolseley.

I was wrong. It wasn't like either: situated on a wide dusty road, it was a small greenish grey building with an old man in something resembling an army uniform standing guard by the glass doors. Gurjit parked up, did his best to hide his disappointment when father told him it would be just the three of us eating. I followed mother out of the nearly-Jeep, took in the heat of the city before stepping into the air conditioned building. The restaurant was medium sized, dark, the lights turned down low to make it perpetually feel like it was 3am, the tables well laid with white table cloths. One of the waiters sat us at a round table meant for four. He handed each of us menus, I didn't open mine, I knew that father would order for all three of us. The waiter took the order of a whole butter chicken, muttar paneer and naan then poured us three glasses of water. Father looked at me.

'Don't drink the water,' he said. 'I'll order some. Do you want to try some Indian beer?'

I nodded. The week and a bit without alcohol had left me parched.

Our seating positions effectively formed an isosceles triangle, with mother and father on the shorter end pointing straight at me. It was a pincer movement of sorts. I wanted to speed things up. I took my napkin and placed it across my lap, then stared straight ahead at the narrow space between them.

'So, I take it you wanted to speak to me about something important,' I said, tensing my stomach muscles like I was about to be punched. Mother made eye contact with father, who blinked his consent for her to talk first.

'Beta, we just wanted to talk about the future,' she said, the level of her voice carefully controlled. 'Now that the house is being built, we are thinking about making our plans to leave Britain.'

'Leave Britain? I thought the plan was to stay there for six months and here for six months?'

'That was the original plan,' father said, 'but having been here for a few weeks, we've been thinking that it would be best to leave Britain behind. We've lived and worked hard in Britain for most of our lives, but it's never been our home. And the more the country goes to the dogs, which it seems to be, year by year, the more we've been thinking that we're better off here. This is the mother country isn't it?'

'The mother country,' I muttered, thinking that I had just said it in my head.

'The house is going to be finished in maybe three or four months,' father continued. 'In that time, I want to retire, secure my pension and savings, and begin the process of moving everything over.'

'Everything,' I said, like I was a wall and the words were just echoing off me. 'But what about me?'

'This is it beta. We've been here to support you all your life. And we don't want that to change,' she paused, reached her hand out to touch mine. 'We don't want to leave you in England. We want you to come and build your life here.'

'Here? But what about my job? What about Anita? She wouldn't leave her job.'

Mother looked at father, it was a look that reminded me of my meeting with Reid and Evrard.

'Son I think you misunderstand us,' father said. 'We only want you to come to India.'

I drank some of the water I wasn't supposed to drink. The waiter had been overwhelmed by three different families arriving for lunch. I really could have done with a beer.

'You want me to leave Anita?'

'We want you to be happy in your work and in your marriage,' mother said, nerves starting to set in. 'We both know that you're not happy with either.'

'But that's no reason to quit it all and leave the country,' I said, feeling some strength in my resolve.

Father leaned forward, 'We've never told you what to do in your life, we've always supported you, but you have to understand that this can't last forever. We're looking at the next stage of our life. We're not sure if we should leave you in Britain.'

'Oh that's it. You don't think I can look after myself.'

They both remained silent, a simple 'yes' would have been less of an answer.

Father was the first to break into what he really wanted to say:

'We never wanted you to marry that little madam, or take that low pay job. You could have earned more working in the Post Office. But you did, and look where it got you. A wife who runs off to her parents, a job where they treat you like a coolie, and no.'

He knew he didn't need to finish the third part. Mother chimed in. She knew it needed to be said.

'Beta, Anita can't have children. It happens sometimes, and it is very sad, but you are still young and have the opportunity to start again.'

I didn't want to consider it, the main reason being because I did want to consider it. Life throws many things at you, but you never really get a chance to start again. Not like this. Seeing that they had got to me, mother moved in for the kill.

'There's a girl here in Jalandhar. A chamari. Very well educated and beautiful. She's training to be a doctor. When she finishes, she could work anywhere.'

The waiter came over with the butter chicken. We waited for him to go, the food steaming before us. I had time to connect the dots.

'That's why those people came to visit. You were trying to arrange my marriage without me even noticing! The girl, what's her name?' I already knew the answer, I wanted mother to say it.

'She wasn't supposed to talk to you last night. That wasn't meant to happen.'

I bit my lip, the swaying of Lakshmi's hips brushing through my mind. I was faltering. Father knew exactly what to say.

'I know this is a lot to take in. All we want you to do is think about it. Believe me, you could have a much happier, fuller life here.'

I was flexing my jaw, father's movement to pick up a naan bread signalling an end to the conversation. Again I was snatching for that brief memory from the previous night, not knowing if it was my mind, heart or groin that was stopping me from ruling out their crazy idea.

Things fall apart. But they often have a way of falling to build something new. I spent the remaining few days of my time in India in my room. In honesty, it was out of shame that I wasn't angrier with them than I should have been. They were my parents. It was true that they had given me everything, and I had given them nothing back in return. They kept silent when I told them I was going to marry Anita. Inside, I knew they were raging, but they let me do it, and they died a little when I told them about the first miscarriage. They cried for her, but they were also crying for themselves. I couldn't blame them for that.

The journey back to Amritsar airport was completed in near silence. We left the village around 8pm, again father up front with Gurjit, the latter turning on the radio because the distance between us all was affecting his concentration. I didn't know if I was saying goodbye to a country I hardly knew. I thought I was, but in fairness I couldn't say it in all certainty.

Amritsar airport was as I remembered: a part finished, beacon of light. The security guards were only letting people with tickets into the building. Father and I stood outside, the mosquitoes getting their last lick. He hugged me in a perfunctory manner, knowing that I craved for so much more.

'Take care of yourself. And call us when you are in Wapping.' He squeezed my shoulders. 'And think. This is your life son, but it is our life too.'

I left him there, looking back and waving before I entered the building. I couldn't be sure, but I think there were tears in his eyes. I only started crying when I had checked in and was in the agonising wait for the plane. I didn't want my parents to leave me, ever.

I slept through most of the flight to London, had broken dreams about love, real love and the love I longed for. I was fortunate not to have to wait for a suitcase. It was always the hardest part of coming home, the wait to make it through immigration, and then the wait for luggage, compounded by the sight of cockroaches running free from the conveyor belts. I breezed through immigration knowing that I would fork out for the Heathrow Express, so I could get home sooner, shower and sleep.

Walking straight out of customs I made a cursory look to see if anyone was waiting for me. It was a habit formed from watching too many Hollywood films. To my surprise, I saw a large card with my name written on it, Anita peering over it. I kissed her on the cheek.

'Why didn't you tell me you were going to meet me,' I said, genuinely pleased to see her. 'I might have walked right past you.'

'Yeah and I would have kicked your ass if you did.'

I kissed her other cheek. There was a brightness in her eyes I hadn't seen for a while, I then realised that she was happy.

'What is it?' I asked.

'I have some news to tell you,' she said. 'I'm pregnant.'

It took me over a week to build up the courage, but I finally set a meeting to discuss my work situation with Reid. He thought it was best if we had our meeting at a nearby cafe. The atmosphere in the office was still tense like a clenched fist, eyes far better than CCTV cameras following every movement when office doors were closed and opened. He went out, then I followed like we were having an affair.

He seemed completely different, when we were sat in the cafe: relaxed, genial, supportive, a small notebook on the table just in case he needed it. We made small talk until our coffees arrived then settled down to business.

'I've worked hard to make my workflow more efficient to fit in the four-day week, but a change in my personal circumstances has made me reassess my situation,' I said. I had written my lines and memorised them the night before.

'Why what's happened? Is everything OK?'

'Anita's pregnant.'

Reid took it in with a nod of his head. I felt like I wouldn't have to say much more.

'Is she doing fine, all . . . checked out?' he asked. He knew about the miscarriages.

I nodded. 'So far all good. You can understand we're being extra cautious. Anita's talking to her boss to see if she can have extended leave so she can go on bed rest, when the pregnancy becomes more advanced. We've got the support of her parents. And I'm sure that my parents will lend a hand, when I tell them.'

He looked like he was going to ask about mother and father, but then changed his mind. He took a sip of coffee, I mirrored his movements.

'Well, I knew this conversation would come. It was just a matter of when. Tarsem, I'm surprised that you took so long.'

'What do you mean?'

'You have to understand that everything is a system. I take orders from my boss, who takes orders from his boss, decisions are made in some boardroom hundreds of miles away. It all just trickles down. The point is that there's always a way to work the system.'

I thought about asking him why he didn't tell me this before, then thought better of it.

'What are you suggesting?' I asked.

'What I'm suggesting is this: you've proved that you can do your picture desk work in four days instead of five, we can't challenge that, but as one of the directors I know that the board is looking to widen the pool of people writing for the magazine. They paid some consultancy agency to look at who's reading our rag. They found that we were missing out on "ethnic minorities" and people over forty. So we have to change to reflect this. Now I'm not sure how you'll feel about this, but considering that you've already written a piece for us, and your ethnicity, there might be a way to wrangle you over to editorial one day a week. HR won't argue, it's just a case of convincing Fenton and his cronies.'

I nodded, not quite sure how I felt about someone playing the race card on my behalf. After another sip of coffee I didn't care. I needed this to happen.

'Do you think I've got a good chance?'

'You've got a better chance than them hiring someone new for five days a week. The editors get to look like they're doing something in response to the consultants, and we finally get someone from production editorial over to content editorial. Doesn't that sound good?'

'Yes, of course.'

'Good,' Reid said, in a way that made it clear that the conversation was over. He said he had to make a few phone calls, so I left him there and went back to the office.

I did my best to hide my delight as I walked back to my desk. I did some work, quelled the urge to text Anita, then thought of Rubina. She had texted me a few days after I arrived back from India. She just wanted to know how it went. I didn't know where to begin. I hadn't replied. I thought about the protest at the library, and going back to her flat, the shame and fear of being caught leading me to search for the photographer and see what photos he had posted online.

I found his portfolio on Flickr, a few clicks later I was in the album of photos from the library protest. There was only one of myself and Rubina sat waiting for the author talk to begin. It's hard to see yourself sometimes. Seeing a photograph of myself sat there was the first time I had seen myself in months, maybe years: my temples had greyed, hair line in a recession of its own, I wasn't the svelte man about town I thought I was. Older than my thirty three years, a guilty expression on my face, heavy creases under my eyes. I had to look away.

The photographer didn't know my name, so there was no way he could tag the photo, no way the web crawlers could find their way to me or Rubina. I closed the browser and carried on working. I needed to use the confidence gained from my meeting with Reid to pluck up the courage to call Rubina. I waited until lunchtime, rang her number on my mobile expecting that she would let it ring through to voicemail. To my surprise she answered almost immediately.

'Hi, how are you?' she said in a positive tone of voice.

'I'm OK. On my lunch break. I wanted to speak to you.'

'You want to meet up? I'm busy tonight, but could probably do tomorrow evening?'

'No, I meant speak now, speak to you now.'

She paused, her tone changing, 'OK, what did you want to say?'

'Anita's pregnant.'

'Oh … I thought—'

'We did, before I left for India. It wasn't planned, it just happened.'

'I'm pleased for you,' she said half-heartedly. 'I really am.'

'I wanted to say that I think it's best if we don't see each other. I need to sort myself out and make sure that I do what's best for her.'

'I understand,' she said, her voice tightening. She needed to change the subject, 'How was India?'

'It was good mostly. Except I think I might have disowned my parents, or they might have disowned me.'

'Disowned! That sounds a bit severe.'

'I don't know where to begin regarding that trip. It was certainly something special.'

'And Anita. Is she OK?'

'She's good. We're all taking extra precautions this time. The doctors seem confident.'

'Good. That's good.' Her voice broke out for a few seconds, I don't know if it was the line or not. 'You know it could have been different.'

It was my time to pause. 'I know. Sometimes I wish it was different. I wish it was all different.'

'Well,' she said trying to sound sanguine, 'at least that's something we will share.'

'Of course.'

'Take care Tarsem. I'll see you around,' she said. I matched her words, then waited for her to hang up.

So here we are.

It's a little after 2am. Your mother is lying here next to me asleep, you are inside her, safe, warm and protected. Anita tells me that she can feel the swelling, the pressure against her pelvis, but you have not yet appeared as a bump in both our lives. But we know that you are there. And in a few weeks' time we will have a scan to prove it, and to be sure that all is well inside.

Since Anita told me, I've found it harder and harder to sleep. I feel exhausted but something inside me tells me that I need to watch, and that I need to talk, to tell you about the things I've done, foolish and selfish as they often have been. They say that you can hear me, even if you can't, at least I am confident that I can hear myself for the first time. I'm not looking for anything, not searching. Everything I need and want is right here. If you can hear me, I hope you are not able yet to judge me. That can wait. If you are a boy, I guess you will love your mother more than me. If you are a girl, I guess I will have my guard up and want to protect you forever.

I need to tell you about your family. You have a brother and a sister. Your brother is called Mohan, he is the eldest, a beautiful boy. Your sister is called Jasmin, which means 'a flower'. I never saw her, but I know that she would be every bit as special and pure as her brother. They are not here like I am, but I am sure that they are watching you all the same. I'm sure that they will be there to guide you into our arms.

I don't know what sort of world you will be entering. We are living in a time where we see war as a thinly veiled scramble for resources, where companies are like countries, free to roam and do as they please, while billions suffer. But there is also hope. There is always hope. For the first time in my generation we have realised that we have to come together, that we have to stand up in whichever way we can, whether it's talking, writing, or marching. Today the Deputy Prime Minister, a man they like to call Clegg, told his wavering support that 'with power comes protest'. Well, now we are going to see if protest can also bring power. I'll be honest and say that I'm not sure if it can, but I do live in hope, because I hope for a better future for you. A future where you will be free from some of the things that me and your mother have lived with.

I don't want to sadden you, but I need to tell you now – and I'm sure I will say this again – that racism and prejudice exist through all walks of life. As much among the educated as the illiterate. It even exists in me. I will try my best to make sure that it does not take seed in you. It is not all bad though. Yesterday I had my first day at the magazine as a trainee editor. My role is going to be to do some writing, mostly for the website, and also some commissioning of longer pieces with the aim to find new journalists. It's a completely different world to picture research, and the pay is not any better, but it has set me free from the call centre. And, although she wouldn't say it, Anita is relieved and expectant that one day I will make the move to being a writer.

Today I also called my parents. They are back from India. We hadn't really spoken until now. I told them about work, that I was making progress and that I wanted to stay in England. They were disappointed but said they understood. I still haven't told them about you. I will. I just want to wait a bit longer. I know they will be happy. I hope they will be happy.

In telling you all this I feel like I've told you the worst of me, many of the things that I am not proud about, but my aim is to spend the rest of my life showing you the best of me. Tomorrow, I'm going to start telling Anita everything I have told you: about Rubina, about work, about India, and about how I feel about her. I don't know what will happen, how she will react. There's no way of telling, occasionally you pull the strings of her heart and she cries, but that isn't your fault. We still go and see the counsellor. He says we're making progress but still have some way to go, which doesn't come as a surprise considering how much we pay him. Anyway, try to forget what I just said.

Anita is stirring in her sleep. I don't want to wake her. I just want to tell you one last thing: whatever happens, I want you to know that you will always be loved. By me, by your mother, by all of the people around you, always. And in that there is protection against any government and any corporation who does you harm by claiming to do the greater good.

I better go to sleep, tomorrow is going to be a long day. Wish me luck dear one. Good night.

AUTHOR'S NOTE

Today is Sunday 10 April 2011. Iceland has rejected a repayment deal to the UK and the *News of the World* has printed an apology for 'voicemail interception'. It is also the day that I finished writing *West of No East*, two days before it is due to go to print to meet the publication date of Tuesday 24 May 2011.

It is rare and in many cases crazy to write a novel, and produce a book in this manner, but I did it because I specifically wanted this story to be as fresh and relevant as it could be. The world has changed, the way news is delivered speeded up, everything is about this very second. Inevitably this poses a problem for writers, especially those trying to write a novel about what is happening right now, whatever that may be.

I had thought about writing *West of No East* for a long time, years even. It is my first published novel, but not the first novel I have written. I'm 32 now, I remember writing a novel when I was 22. By my own admission it was so bad that I conveniently forgot to back it up, when I switched to a new computer. I'm pretty sure I've done a better job with this one, but I guess time will tell, when I reread it in a few months' time.

The events of the last few years have focussed my thoughts on the nature of protest, and, more importantly, the mechanics of change. I wanted to situate a story, which is in essence a love story of sorts, against a very real backdrop of events. Chronologically the story begins in November 2010 and ends on 12 March 2011. I had to alter the timeline a little to fit in the library day of protest, which actually came when Tarsem was supposed to be in India. I know someone will notice, but I hope it doesn't matter.

From those dates you can sort of tell that I have finished this novel about a month later than I was supposed to. What can I say? Life intervened.

It is inevitable that readers will think that this story is autobiographical, which it is and clearly is not – this is the nature of writing. I have not experienced a lot of the things that Tarsem experiences, I hope I have done them enough justice. When it comes to the notion of autobiography, I defer to Kundera's *The Art of the Novel*, in which he wrote that an author is merely exploring possibilities, things that could happen, but never really have. That's what I like to say. Those who know me will have their opinions, those who don't know me can have a fun time trying to guess.

I will finish writing for now. I have to print this out, do a very quick edit, and proof the spreads – again a very unorthodox and an unadvisable way of doing things, but I never set out to start a publishing house and write a novel in an orthodox way. The final thing I will say is that the title of this novel is inspired by Charles Bukowski's *South of No North*. Wherever he is, I really hope he doesn't mind.

— Bobby Nayyar

A GLASSHOUSE BOOKS PUBLICATION

Design by Eren Butler
Written by Bobby Nayyar
Typeset in Arno Pro and Chalet Comprime Cologne Sixty
First published 24. 05. 2011

ISBN 978-1-907536-32-8

Glasshouse Books
58 Glasshouse Fields
Flat 30, London
E1W 3AB

glasshousebooks.co.uk
facebook.com/GlasshouseBooks
Printed and bound in Great Britain by Clays Ltd, St Ives PLC

GLASSHOUSE BOOKS 2011 TITLES

WEST OF NO EAST

MEN & WOMEN

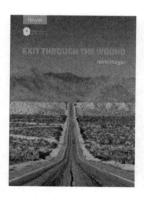

EXIT THROUGH THE WOUND

FREELANCER'S DIARY 12

Me. You. Everyone.

glasshousebooks.co.uk